The Chocolate Touch

The Chocolate Touch

A Love at the Chocolate Shop Romance

Melissa McClone

TULE
PUBLISHING

Dedication

For everyone who hangs out on the Love at the Chocolate
Shop Facebook page!

Acknowledgements

Thanks to Air Force Colonel Mike Cannon (Ret.) and Mrs. Beth Cannon, Air Force veteran.

Special thanks to Kimberly Field, Tina Jones, Terri Reed, Melanie Snitker, and Melissa Storm for their support and friendship.

Chocolate expert Chantelle Cummings arrives in Marietta, Montana with two goals—sign copies of her new book and research a quaint local chocolate shop. When she meets a gorgeous guy passing out chocolate samples, her visit turns sweeter than she ever imagined. The man melts her heart, but her dream of working in France with her family makes her hesitant to pursue a romance.

Former Air Force captain York Parker has one month before embarking upon a consulting career. He never expected to be selling chocolates, but he's happy to help his sister and her boss. He also likes spending time with sassy, pretty Chantelle. His new coworker may have the chocolate touch, but he'd rather taste her decadent kisses… until he learns the real reason she's in town.

Will the truth harden his heart, or will love pave the way to a sweet future?

Chapter One

WALKING INTO PARADISE Books in Marietta, Montana, York Parker was a man with a mission. He might not be a captain in the air force any longer, but he was the big brother of two incredible women—Dakota and Nevada—and one needed his help tonight. He was used to scanning code on his computer screen and watching trajectories on monitors, so he went into surveillance mode to find Dakota.

Rows of chairs and a wooden podium suggested a reading or some other event had taken place recently, maybe tonight, but his sister wasn't there. She also wasn't among the bookcases or with the customers who stood in a line along the left-hand side of the store.

Where could she be?

The place wasn't that big.

Someone crashed into his back, and he took a step to maintain his balance. He was fine, but he couldn't say the same about the person clinging to his left arm and shoulder like a dead weight.

"Oh, no." The voice was feminine and breathy. "I'm so sorry. I wasn't paying attention to where I was going."

"That's okay." And man, was it.

Soft curves pressed against York. The scent of vanilla surrounded him. He couldn't see her face, but everything else about her was near perfect. *If* he were looking for a hookup.

Which he wasn't.

He went into big-brother mode, turned, and put his free hand on her waist to help her balance. "Are you hurt?

"No, just a big ball of nerves." She straightened, and he missed her warmth and scent. "Though don't tell anyone I said that please."

"Your secret is safe with me." He took a good look at her.

Hello, gorgeous.

She was in her mid-to-late twenties with a beautiful face that could stop a convoy of Humvees and long, blond hair that belonged spread over a pillow or a man's chest.

Like his.

York's pulse kicked up a notch. Okay, more than one.

She wore a pale blue above-the-knee skirt and matching jacket. Attractive and well dressed. A combination that was hard to resist.

"Thanks, but..." A big, blue-eyed gaze—the color of the sky on this fine day in May—met his.

His breath caught in his throat. Something twisted in his gut. He stared, captivated.

Not the reaction he was expecting, nor like anything he'd felt while charming scantily clad women on the beach last week.

"Did I hurt you?" she added.

Reality returned in an instant. He bit back a laugh. If she could hurt him, he needed serious help. She was average height to his six-two. Not skinny by any means. She had curves a man could hold onto or sink into. Just his type. And too small to do much damage to someone as big as him by accident… or even if she'd tried.

But he heard her concern and appreciated that she knew she was the one at fault. "I'm fine, Miss…?"

York wanted to know her name.

"Good." She glanced around the store instead. "I need to find the restroom. Do you know where it is?"

"Sorry, first time in here."

"Well, I'd better keep looking. Thanks for keeping me from hitting the floor. That would have been more embarrassing."

"No need to be embarrassed. You can bump into me anytime."

With a quick smile flashed in his direction, she hurried away.

The sway of her hips and heels that showed off her long legs had him watching her go. He didn't get her name, but that was probably for the best.

"York. Thank goodness you're here."

He turned toward the sound of his sister's voice. She stood by an artful display of chocolates that had been set up on a large, rectangle table.

"You called for help," he said. "I got here as soon as I could."

Dakota wore her work uniform—indigo blue shirt, dark jeans, and a copper-colored apron. Her light brown hair was pulled back into a French braid. She looked the same as when she'd left the house at nine-thirty this morning. Not surprising since she hadn't been home. He and their sister Nevada had been there to let out the dog this afternoon. No reason for Dakota to come back on her lunch break.

She placed chocolates on a white platter. Wearing plastic gloves didn't slow her down, but she'd worked at Copper Mountain Chocolates for almost four years. She was an expert at this, and loved her job selling chocolates. He'd be getting a first-hand look at what she did when he filled in at the shop for a couple of her coworkers.

A smile spread across her face. "I knew I could count on you."

The relief in her voice made him glad he'd arrived quickly. The dark lines under her brown eyes, however, bothered him. She'd worked a full day at the chocolate shop and was now at the bookstore. She had to be tired. Yesterday on her day off, she'd volunteered at the Whiskers and Paw Pals Animal Rescue. Only two hours, but still…

"What's going on?" he asked.

"I told you Portia's baby is due at the end of the month."

Portia was one of his sister's co-workers at the chocolate shop. He hadn't met her yet. "Is she okay?"

"I think so. She was supposed to work tonight. When she arrived, she looked exhausted. I sent her home to rest. Sage's kids have fevers so she couldn't be here, either. And Rosie is in LA. That's why I need your help. This is a two-person job." Dakota handed him a copper-colored apron like the one she wore. "Here."

He grinned. "This doesn't look like my SuperBro cape."

"Capes are overrated. And you'll be wearing one just like this when you work at the shop tomorrow. Put it on, bro."

He did and was happy to do whatever she needed.

Dakota and Nevada were the reasons he was spending the month in Marietta. What better place to be than with his sisters before he started traveling nonstop with his new job as a computer consultant? Being here also gave him time to check out their respective boyfriends—Bryce Grayson and Dustin Decker. York wanted to make sure the guys were as wonderful as his sisters claimed.

He planned to use Dakota's place as a home base after his job started since he would be traveling and not around much. If he determined he needed a better location to live, he would move.

She gave him a once-over, and the corners of her mouth turned downward. "Your hair is wet."

"I grabbed a quick shower before I drove over. Didn't

think you wanted me showing up without one after replacing windows all day. Too dirty and sweaty."

"You're right, good call, but you didn't have time to shave?"

"Nope." York tied the strings around his back. He didn't realize the chocolate shop had such high appearance standards. He'd better come clean on one more fault. "I also couldn't find an iron."

Her smile returned. "That's because I don't own one."

What? And why did she sound so proud about that fact?

No matter. He knew what to get Dakota for her birthday.

"You're not in the air force any longer," she said. "A couple of wrinkles won't hurt you."

York was adjusting to being a civilian. He kept thinking he was on leave, but once he was working full time, he'd stop thinking that way. "Don't let Mom hear you say that."

Growing up, their mom ironed everything from bedsheets to T-shirts.

"At least the colonel's not here to ground us if we're wrinkled," he added.

The colonel was York's nickname for their father who'd retired from the army. A name York had never called the man to his face.

"I hated when Dad did that." Dakota made a face. "Though you appreciated the extra time to play on your computer, and Nevada loved being able to read more."

Neither of those things had appealed to Dakota due to her reading disability.

"But no kid deserved to be treated like a trainee in boot camp," she continued.

Forget the iron. York would get his sister something else for her birthday. "True, but Dad didn't know any other way."

And the three of them hadn't turned out too badly.

York smoothed the front of the apron and then struck a pose. "How do I look?"

"Nice." Dakota's brown eyes twinkled. "The copper color brings out your tan and your blond highlights."

Both were due to spending last week in Fiji on an all-expenses-paid dream vacation courtesy of Nevada's boyfriend, Dustin Decker. Except...

"Not highlights," York corrected. "Sun streaks."

"Same thing."

He shook his head. "No salon visits or spa days for this guy. The colonel would kill me if I did anything like that."

Dakota returned to putting chocolates on the platter. "Maybe sailing around the Caribbean has mellowed him."

York might be thirty-two, but his father was still this larger-than-life, all-knowing figure. One who was a tad intimidating, but that hadn't stopped York from leaving the air force when the colonel wanted him to reenlist. His father had liked the stability and security of being career military, but earning retirement benefits didn't make up for the daily routine and lack of control over the future. No way could York keep doing it for another ten or twenty years.

"Let's hope so." A sigh welled up inside York. He hadn't spoken to his parents since he'd gone to Fiji. "What can I do to help? Taste chocolate?" York asked in a hopeful tone.

"You can do that at the shop tomorrow." Dakota handed him a pair of plastic gloves. "Tonight, you're going to pass out chocolates."

He made a sad face. "None for me?"

"You can have any leftovers," she said in that patient voice she used with her many foster animals. Her current menagerie consisted of an old, gray-faced dog named Fang and a sleeps-all-day cat named Sapphire, who would go to her forever home tomorrow. "Though there might not be much left with this crowd. Marietta loves Sage's chocolate."

"Me, too."

Sage Carrigan O'Dell owned Copper Mountain Chocolates. He'd met her the last time he was in town. A nice woman.

York put on the gloves.

Dakota looked at the line of customers against the far wall. "More people are here than expected. I'll prepare another tray and pour hot chocolate samples."

"You're going all out."

"All of our events are important, but this one is...special." She double-checked the platter. "Be sure to smile."

"When I'm around chocolate and you, smiling happens naturally."

Dakota beamed. "You're the best brother."

He couldn't let her words go without saying something. "I'm your only brother."

She stuck out her tongue at him.

That made York laugh. He missed her. And Nevada, too. Spending a few days with them during the holidays wasn't enough.

Being a big brother meant looking out for his sisters and teasing them, too. Dakota and Nevada meant more to him than anything. Yes, they could push his buttons, but he could press theirs right back. That was what being siblings was all about.

Growing up, he'd worn sparkly tiaras and pink boas, attended more tea parties than he could count, let his sisters cry on his shoulder, and taken care of the jerks who broke their hearts.

Who was he kidding?

He still did those things—minus wearing the crowns and feathers. Although, he would if they needed him to.

He picked up the platter. "Looks like I'm good to go."

Dakota dragged her upper teeth across her lower lip.

Funny, but their mom did the same thing. He'd never noticed his sister doing it, too.

"Keep Chantelle's plate full of chocolate," Dakota said. "We want her to fall in love with Sage's special recipes."

Chantelle was a name he hadn't heard before. "Who?"

"The author. Chantelle Cummings." Dakota's voice held a hint of awe. "She gave a talk earlier, and now she's signing her book *The Chocolate Touch*."

The title explained why Copper Mountain Chocolates was catering the event, but… "Never heard of her. Or the book."

"Shh." Dakota looked around as if to see if anyone heard him. "Chantelle's an expert in the industry. Her book is a collection of reviews and articles she's written about the chocolate from the shops she's visited. A positive review from her can bring in customer orders from all over the world."

"Sage seems to be doing well on her own."

"Yes, but new customers keep a business growing. Can you imagine if Cooper Mountain Chocolates made it into Chantelle's next book?"

Based on Dakota's excited tone, that would be a big deal. "I'll make sure the plate is full."

His words seemed to appease his sister.

"Sage invited Chantelle to tomorrow night's tasting, but we don't know if she'll attend." Dakota handed him a stack of small napkins. "When you interact with her or anyone, please be my charming brother. Not my annoying one."

Come on. She had to know he wouldn't do anything to embarrass her.

He grinned. "I'm only annoying when it's you, Nevada, and me."

York walked to the end of the line. That seemed like the best place to start since these people had to wait the longest to meet the author whose name he'd forgotten. He handed out pieces with a smile. A few people he recognized from his past visits, but most he didn't. His last visit to Marietta had been over two years ago.

The size of the crowd, however, surprised him. Marietta residents must either support their local businesses or be addicted to Sage's chocolates.

Maybe both given how fast the platter was emptying.

When he reached the front of the line, only four chocolates remained. So much for leftovers that he could eat. Oh, well. Maybe there'd be more left with the next round.

Laughter—a sweet, almost melodic sound—caught his attention. York looked over. He did a double-take.

The woman sitting at a table stacked with books was the same one who had bumped into him. She spoke to an older woman with gray hair who stood on the opposite side of the table.

That must be the author.

Her smile was warm and genuine. He could tell she liked speaking to people about her book. Passion gleamed in her eyes.

Passion for chocolate.

Or more...?

Awareness hummed through him, followed by a rush of anticipation.

Uh-oh. He'd better stop staring. Dakota had told him to keep the author's plate full—it wasn't. But he remembered how she felt against him—how she smelled—and that was more of a turn-on than he wanted to admit even to himself.

York made his way to the right-hand side of the table. The author didn't glance his way. She was preoccupied signing a book. He would wait for the right time to refill her plate.

He glanced at the book's cover.

Chantelle. That was the name he'd forgotten.

A photograph of two chocolates on a plain white plate was on the front. He would have rather seen a woman holding a piece of chocolate, or, better yet, putting a piece into her mouth. Chantelle Cummings had nice, full lips.

As the older woman walked away, he picked up one of the chocolates with his gloved hand and placed the piece on Chantelle's plate.

She jumped. "What are you doing?"

"Giving you more chocolate."

Eyes wide, she looked at him as if he'd grown horns and smelled like Big Foot. Then she relaxed. "Oh, it's you."

He took her remembering him as a good sign. Maybe she didn't make a habit of splaying herself over strangers.

"I'm sorry if I startled you," he said. "But it was my turn."

She laughed. "That's true, and you were nicer than me."

He raised a brow. "How's that?"

"You didn't make me catch you."

Okay, she had a sense of humor. That was good, too.

"What do you have for me?" she asked.

Ten lines ran through his mind. He could come up with many more. Not one he could use on her now, though.

"You won't find better chocolate in Montana." He might as well sell the product because that was what Dakota would do, and this was what he'd be expected to do when he filled in at the shop. "What other pieces would you like?"

Chantelle's gaze traveled from him to the three chocolates on the platter. "What's your favorite?"

York heard a challenge in her question. For someone who seemed a bit of a klutz and out of sort a few minutes ago, she seemed to pull herself together quickly.

His smile didn't waver, even though he didn't know the names of the pieces. "All are good."

That sounded like a safe answer that wouldn't get him or Dakota into trouble.

"What kind of truffles are those?" Chantelle asked.

Truffles? He glanced at the platter. Two pieces were rounded. Those must be the truffles, but he had no idea of the flavors. The square one had salt on top so it might be a caramel.

He'd try a logical answer. "Chocolate."

Chantelle eyed him as if she knew his secret. Her mouth quirked. "You don't know what they're called, do you?"

"No." He'd gotten out of more than one tight spot by

keeping his cool and a smile on his face. "I'm helping out my sister tonight. But even if I don't know the names, my tastes buds don't care. Everything Sage makes is delicious."

A beat passed. And another. She gazed into his eyes. Hers were questioning. Curious.

Time seemed to stop. He felt as if he were floating in the pools of blue. The feeling didn't suck.

She looked away. "You've convinced me."

That was easy, but Chantelle's matter of fact tone didn't tell him whether she was amused or annoyed with him. Given the way her gaze flickered from him to the line of autograph seekers, he'd say the latter.

"I'll take all three, please," she added.

York placed the remaining pieces on her plate. He liked that she didn't hold back on the chocolates. "You're a woman who knows what she wants."

The wariness returned to her eyes, but she wouldn't look at him. She seemed more interested in everything else in the store besides him, and he wished she'd go back to being a 'ball of nerves' as she'd put it.

"When it comes to chocolate, yes," she said.

"That's because you have the chocolate touch."

Chantelle pressed her lips together. She looked like a completely different person from the one who had bumped into him.

"Heard that line before?" he asked.

"Many times."

Too many based on the hard set of her jaw. Probably too late for damage control, but he'd try. "Then I won't ask you about chocolate kisses or anything else."

"Good. Otherwise, I'd have to invoke the chocolate curse."

"Curse? You've piqued my curiosity."

"Sorry. Top secret."

He had a security clearance. Or did and would again once he started his new consulting job. But that wasn't something he'd tell a stranger, even a beautiful one who probably wore fancy, lacy lingerie.

Whoa.

Where did that come from?

He'd better get out of there before he said something inappropriate.

"Your plate's full. My job is done." He didn't want to embarrass Dakota or himself. "I'll let you get back to signing books."

"Champagne and mocha." The words rushed out of Chantelle's mouth.

"Excuse me?"

"Those are the two flavors of truffles you gave me. There's also a dark chocolate salted caramel, and the first thing you put on my plate is a toffee."

She spoke fast. That breathy tone was back. Confidence in a woman was a sexy trait, but he liked seeing her less in control.

"One out of four isn't bad." He half-laughed. "I guessed one was caramel due to the salt."

His gaze met hers.

Something passed between them. A look, but not like before. This was more of a…connection.

Forget acting like a big brother with this one.

A spark raced up his arm even though they hadn't touched. The flash of hunger in her eyes made York think she'd like a taste of him, too.

He wouldn't mind a nibble. "Enjoy them."

"I will. And thanks for catching me."

"Anytime."

"I'm not a klutz."

"Did I say you were?"

"No, but…" She bit her lip.

He was tempted to put his mouth there. Really tempted.

But people were waiting to speak with her and get their books signed. He was out of chocolate and needed a new platter. Still, his feet didn't want to move.

There'd been energy—chemistry—in that look. Heat, too. Enough to intrigue him and send his temperature rising, both before and now. He had gotten enough of a feel of her body to want to touch her again. The only thing he risked was rejection, and he'd never let that stop him before.

Until he remembered his reason for being in Marietta.

Two reasons.

Dakota and Nevada.

He wasn't in Fiji anymore.

A vacation romance wasn't on his radar.

He had a month before his computer consultant job started, and then he'd have to travel to wherever clients needed him. He'd be living out of a suitcase with no vacation time. He wanted to make the most of his time in Marietta.

Family time.

Holding onto the empty platter, he walked away, forcing himself not to look back at the beautiful author with the chocolate touch.

His sisters were the priority this month.

No one else.

Chapter Two

AFTER THE BOOK signing, Chantelle returned to her room at the Graff Hotel. Being in the suite soothed her. She hadn't expected a small town to offer such luxurious accommodations, and she loved the combination of Old World and modern décor.

The king-sized bed called to her—so did her pajamas—but first things first.

Her feet hurt from a combination of swelling from her flight and her shoes. She kicked off her heels.

Relief.

She wiggled her toes in the plush carpet.

Now it was time to relax.

Her tight muscles needed to loosen, and her insides...

She needed to stop feeling so unsettled. A feeling that had nothing to do with traveling all day, or being at the book signing, or finding herself in a new place.

Then I won't ask you about chocolate kisses or anything else.

He'd unsettled her. The nameless guy whose fit, hard body had nearly sent her tumbling to the ground. His gaze had been full of interest, but he hadn't taken advantage of the situation. No groping when he'd helped her straighten. His touch had been a strange combination—gentle yet firm—and set off an explosion of tingles and twitches from her nerve endings. She'd like the way that felt even if her brain short-circuited from the contact. He might be clueless about chocolate, but he was a tasty piece of eye candy.

Attractive.

Okay, hot.

His wide shoulders emphasized his athletic build. Not muscle bound—though she'd felt the ridges and firmness beneath his shirt—but enough definition to make her mouth water as if the perfect piece of eighty-five percent dark chocolate had fallen from the sky. His tan face and sun-streaked hair suggested he spent time outdoors—for fun, work, or both? The scruff of whiskers made her wonder if they'd scratch or tickle against her skin. Add in smoldering hazel eyes, and she hadn't been so attracted to someone at first glance in… well, she couldn't remember when.

Her reaction wasn't typical. She'd met good-looking men during her travels. Some had bought her drinks and others had taken her out to dinner, but none had affected her quite this way. Chantelle had wanted him to come back and talk to her more, not ignore her for the rest of the evening.

But ignore her, he did.

She blew out a breath.

She'd kept hoping he'd return to refill her plate, but he

stayed busy passing out the to-die-for chocolates and cups of delicious hot chocolate to everyone else.

Talk about frustrating, even if she wasn't sure why she felt that way.

The woman wearing a similar apron as the guy had re-filled Chantelle's plate the next time. After the event, she'd looked for him. Her excuse was to thank him for catching her earlier so she could find out his name, but he was nowhere around.

She knew he hadn't just vanished. Her only info on him was that he was someone's brother. Was his sister the woman working the chocolate table who had introduced herself when Chantelle first arrived at the bookstore?

Decker or Dakota. Something like that.

Chantelle had been nervous about the event and forgot-ten the woman's name. She didn't feel right asking her about the guy. She hadn't been sure what to say.

Who was the guy in the matching apron?

What's the name of the guy who refilled my plate?

Is that cute guy giving out chocolates single?

Not one question was appropriate.

And neither were her thoughts now.

He was a total stranger. One she couldn't stop thinking about, but so what if she liked his looks and the way he touched her? She needed to stop. Finding a date wasn't on her list of things to do in Marietta.

Besides, she wanted a forever kind of love, not a fling

while passing through a town in the middle of nowhere Montana. That guy had trouble written all over him. She didn't know if he was a player or not, but she needed to stop thinking about him and sleep.

A few minutes later, she'd brushed her teeth and slipped into pajamas. She wasn't going to set her alarm. No reason to when her body was on East Coast time, three hours ahead. She pulled back the bedcovers.

Her cell phone rang. Odd, this late.

She checked her phone. The name Philippe Delacroix glowed on the screen.

Why was her cousin calling from France at this hour?

Her muscles bunched tighter.

Had she done something wrong? Made a mistake?

Chantelle bit her lower lip and plopped onto the bed.

The phone rang again.

She didn't know Philippe that well—she'd only met him once in person—but patience didn't seem to be one of his virtues based on his calls and texts. He kept in touch almost daily, which she appreciated, but the last thing she needed was for him to complain about her to his father.

Her uncle Laurent was not only the head of the family, but he also held the key to her working at Delacroix Chocolates, the award-winning luxurious chocolate company founded by her late grandfather, Pacôme Delacroix. That was her dream job.

Her goal.

And the main reason she was in Marietta.

She'd better take the call. "Hello?"

"Already in bed?" Philippe asked. It wasn't yet seven AM in France, but Philippe was always on the go.

"Not yet, but soon."

She couldn't afford to mess up with the Delacroix family.

Not like her late mother had when she'd married Chantelle's father—an American backpacking around Europe after graduating college—without permission and then been disowned, even though she'd been the one trained by her father to be the company's next chocolatier. Chantelle's mother had died when she was twelve, and she'd never met her mother's side of the family until after her father died while she was in college. He hadn't liked the way the Delacroix family treated her mother, and they hadn't cared enough to stay in touch.

Although she managed to graduate on time thanks to a surprise scholarship she'd been awarded, her grief and tears wouldn't stop. Chantelle didn't like being alone and having no one to call family. She'd gotten in touch with her uncle, who'd then invited her to visit them in Bayonne, France.

The time there had been slightly awkward given they were strangers and no one had reached out to her before, but she'd toured the factory, gone sightseeing, and met her long-lost relatives. She'd even made one of her mother's chocolate recipes for them. The day she left, her uncle suggested she learn as much as she could about the chocolate industry so she could take her rightful place at Delacroix Chocolates. He'd given her a list of steps she needed to do as part of an unofficial apprenticeship and offered to pay her tuition to her choice of any culinary programs.

She'd attended a well-known chocolate academy, and then expanded a blog called Chocolate with Chantelle that she'd started in college. Soon, she was selling articles to food and travel magazines, visiting chocolate shops, writing reviews, and being invited to speak. She'd been working hard since then, while trying to complete all the steps.

All as Chantelle Cummings.

No one knew her connection to one of the most famous chocolate brands in the world. She'd done that on purpose so people, especially her uncle, wouldn't think she was trying to cash in on the family name. It was why any bio, including the one in her book, didn't mention Delacroix Chocolate or the family at all, even though that might have helped her.

Her mother had shared stories about working in the chocolate laboratory and about the luxurious chateau where she'd grown up. It was a fairy-tale worthy life, which was why her mother's family had thought Royce Cummings was after Marie Delacroix's fortune, not in love with her, but that hadn't been the case. True love had conquered all, but caused a decades-long family rift.

Chantelle didn't want her uncle to think she was a fortune hunter. She wasn't in this for money or prestige. She just wanted to belong and be a part of the family. But accomplishing that meant being professional and competent, not getting flustered when she couldn't find a bathroom or bumped into a hot guy like she had earlier.

"Are you still there?" Philippe's English had only a slight French accent. He'd attended school in the United States.

"Yes, I am."

"How did the book signing go?" he asked.

"Sold out."

"Excellent. I'll let Father know."

"Thanks." She didn't know if book sales would sway Uncle Laurent's opinion of her, but she hoped he was proud. Writing a book hadn't been one of the steps on his list, but she figured extra credit wouldn't hurt. "I didn't expect such a large turnout, but the bookstore was packed with customers. Oh, and Copper Mountain Chocolates provided refreshments."

"And?"

The anticipation in Philippe's voice made Chantelle smile. She was tempted to make a joke, but her cousin seemed to be all business and might not appreciate the humor.

"How was it?" Philippe asked.

It.

As if two letters could ever describe the wonderfulness of chocolate.

"The truffles were melt-in-your-mouth delicious. Mind you, the flavor choices were basic, but the quality was impeccable. I can see why their hot chocolate is a top seller. Rich and creamy, yet simple with only a few ingredients. Pure deliciousness in a cup."

"That's what I hoped to hear," Philippe admitted. "Is there anything you didn't like?"

"Too much sea salt on the dark chocolate caramel, but that's an easy fix. Otherwise, nothing glaring stood out."

"Does this mean your first impression is favorable?" His inflection rose at the end.

She preferred to submit a report rather than provide details over the phone as she didn't want anything passed on that she hadn't exactly meant. That had happened the first time she researched a small-batch chocolate producer in Vermont for her uncle.

"First impression is a bit of a misnomer since I haven't been in the shop," she said. "But the chocolates looked and tasted better than I expected."

"Let's hope everything at the shop is even better, because Father is eager to acquire more recipes. He'd like to offer a new collection of chocolates—perhaps call it Americana, although a trendier name might appeal more to a younger demographic."

Good plan. Delacroix Chocolates, though famous, was relying on their long-held reputation and traditional recipes. Delicious yes, but the company needed new products to complement their classic collections to stay fresh and compete with the other high-end chocolate makers. According to

Philippe, expanding the US market share was key to their strategic plans. Though she didn't understand why their chocolatier, an older man named Claude, couldn't come up with them instead of having Uncle Laurent purchase recipes.

"That means we need to find them fast," Philippe added.

We.

Her spine went ramrod straight as she let the word sink in. Her hope was to be living and working in France by summertime, but a delay of a few months didn't matter as long as she ended up there eventually.

For that to happen, Chantelle had to continue to prove her worth to Delacroix Chocolates and the family. She would do anything it took.

Being on her own was hard. And lonely.

"Just let me know what you need," she said.

"You've been an excellent resource already," Philippe said. "You'll be here in Bayonne before you know it."

Yes! Chantelle shimmied her shoulders. She missed her parents and wanted nothing more than to be part of a family again. Soon. "Happy to help."

"Call me after you visit the shop."

"The tasting isn't until the evening."

"Then email me."

"Sounds good." She stifled a yawn. Traveling from the East Coast and being "on" for the signing was making it hard to stay awake.

Philippe disconnected the call without saying goodbye.

Not unusual for him, but she hoped that changed eventually. She also wished they could talk about more than just chocolate one day. He was the closest thing she had to a sibling. Still, she had no complaints. Her plans seemed to be on track.

Contentment settled over her.

Chantelle had a feeling everything she'd dreamed about was finally within her grasp. Wriggling her toes, she grinned. She couldn't wait.

THE NEXT DAY, sunlight streamed through her window, but she wasn't tempted to explore Marietta. Chantelle stayed in her room to write Monday's blog post based on her notes from a tasting she'd attended, and then she drafted an article about pairing wine with chocolate for a food magazine.

Words flowed until lunch arrived via room service. After that, she wrote until it was time to do a phone interview with a Denver radio station about her book.

Yes, people have told her she has the chocolate touch.

No, she doesn't give chocolate kisses.

Her favorite chocolate is whatever she's eating at the time.

Of course chocolate is good for one's health, especially dark chocolate.

She could answer the questions in her sleep because she heard the same ones each time, but her publicist claimed doing interviews would spur book sales so Chantelle kept answering them over again. Not that she minded. She loved talking about chocolate almost as much as she enjoyed eating it.

Bells chimed from her phone.

She'd set her alarm so she'd remember the chocolate tasting. Once she got working, she lost track of time. A trait her father had said she'd inherited from her mother. She wanted to be more like her. Marie Delacroix Cummings had been loving and kind. She also made the most amazing chocolates ever.

A glance in the mirror told Chantelle something was missing from her outfit. None of her necklaces looked good with the chunky earrings she wore, so she tied a scarf around her neck. That looked better and more in line with what a Delacroix would wear. With her purse and jacket in hand, she headed out of her room.

A uniformed valet held open the front door. "Have a wonderful evening."

"Thanks." She flashed a smile in his direction, and then she stepped outside.

The sun was disappearing. A slight breeze blew, but nothing that made her want to put on her coat. She might need it for her walk home after the tasting, but the temperature now was springtime pleasant.

She crossed Front Avenue, walked along First Street, and then turned left on Main Street. Quaint-looking shops lined both sides of the street. Parking was readily available, and the sidewalks were empty. Few cars were on the road.

Hmm. A slow time or was this normal for the time of day? She'd been so focused on getting to the bookstore on time yesterday she hadn't noticed. That was one more thing on her list to check out.

Her uncle had started off by offering to buy small shops in tourist towns to rebrand as Delacroix stores. The shop's recipes would be used to breathe new life into the Delacroix line.

Chantelle had thought this was a good strategy. The purchase offers were above market value and allowed the owners to continue working as Delacroix employees or leave the chocolate business if they so desired. Her uncle, however, hadn't counted on tourists wanting to purchase local products, so he was no longer interested in the shops themselves, only their recipes.

Up ahead on her left was Copper Mountain Chocolates. As she opened the door to the shop, a bell jingled. Familiar smells hit—cocoa and spices. The scent of vanilla was strong, along with a hint of cinnamon and so much more.

She inhaled.

The aroma was delicious and soothing. It brought back memories of home when her mom would make chocolates in the kitchen and let Chantelle help. Each time they made one together, she wrote down her mother's recipes and helpful hints in her diary with a lock that didn't quite work. A warm feeling flowed through her. She'd forgotten much about her mom over the years, but she remembered the chocolate.

"Welcome to Copper Mountain Chocolates. I'm Dakota." The woman standing in front of a glass display case had been the one at the bookstore.

Chantelle silently repeated the woman's name. "Nice to see you again, Dakota."

Now maybe Chantelle would remember the name.

Dakota wore clothes similar to the ones she had on last night—an indigo-blue shirt, jeans, and a copper apron. Her hair was pulled back in a high ponytail, and her eyes were a gold-brown color. Not hazel like the hottie passing out chocolate at the bookstore last night. But her coloring was close to his.

Was this the eye candy's sister?

Must be. Chantelle hadn't seen any other chocolate shop employees at the bookstore last night, but she wasn't here to ask about the woman's brother.

Time to push distractions aside and focus.

She studied the display case. Inside, chocolates were stacked in pyramids on plates. A few items had been decorated with pastel color swirls or coatings. There was quite a variety—from truffles to caramels. A nice dash of color with some of the other spring-themed varieties made the whole display aesthetically pleasing.

On top of the case, flower-shaped molded chocolates filled colorful vases. Perfect for spring and the upcoming Mother's Day. Black-and-white photos of the chocolate process hung on the wall behind the display case. The pictures were artistic and professional.

Dakota stepped forward. "I'm so happy you decided to join us for the tasting."

Her mannerisms suggested she was the friendly type, a nice woman who would deliver soup and chocolate to those she cared about.

"Chocolate tastings are one of my favorite things." Chantelle meant that. Tonight, she could taste and do research at the same time.

"Mine, too." Dakota's smile brightened her pretty face. "Please take a seat. We'll be starting shortly."

"Thank you." Chantelle glanced to her right where people sat at small tables. A few spots remained. "Is there assigned seating?"

"No. You can sit wherever you'd like."

As she looked around again, the shop's décor brought a sense of relief. Some stores were more whimsical or old fashioned. Not this one. The cocoa-and-vanilla-inspired colors brought chocolate to mind. Purely intentional on the owner's part. Smart. Shops like this one not only sold chocolate, but also provided a chocolate experience.

Wood shelves along the far wall added warmth and a place to display products. The copper boxes added a bit of gleam and bling to the otherwise neutral shop. Nice branding, too.

Each chocolate shop she visited was different, but this one impressed her. Copper Mountain Chocolate was designed for repeat customers as well as tourists. The feel, however, was completely opposite from that of a Delacroix Chocolate shop where luxurious and rich described the décor and the product that was sold in a light blue-and-gold keepsake box.

One thing, however, was wrong with this place.

The tables.

Six tables were three too many. There was hardly room to move. Less space to display products. Such a waste.

Unless this layout was only for special events. She would return tomorrow during normal business hours to see if it looked different.

Now…where to sit?

Three of the tables were occupied. Two were half full. One had a man typing on his cell phone. He wore a forest-green polo shirt that contrasted nicely with his sun-streaked brown hair.

Good looking enough that she took a second look.

And this time, she recognized him.

He was the guy from last night. Only he wasn't wearing an apron. And he'd shaved.

The scruff had given him a sexy, bad-boy edge, but she had to admit the smooth skin was just as appealing.

He looked up from his phone and caught her staring at him. His shirt brought out a green tint to his hazel eyes.

Since it was too late to look away, she smiled instead.

He grinned back. "We meet again."

A simple greeting, but her tongue felt big and heavy.

Stop overreacting, she chided herself. He'd greeted her, not flirted. "Hi."

"I don't think I introduced myself last night. I'm York Parker."

"Chantelle Cummings." She caught herself, blushing. "But you know that."

Another nod. He motioned to the three empty chairs at his table. "There's room if you'd like to join me."

York didn't look like a man who had to go anywhere without a date. "Are you expecting anyone else?"

He shook his head. "One sister is working the tasting. My other sister and her boyfriend had tickets, but they stayed home with the new foster that arrived today."

"Foster child?"

"Cat. His name is Zip, and the poor little guy is afraid of every noise and movement. If he's not in the closet, he's under the bed."

Chantelle had never had a pet growing up. She never thought about having one now, either. Not with how much she traveled. Once she was settled, she would get a dog or a cat. Maybe one of each.

York pulled out the chair next to him.

She sat.

Pencils and sheets of papers sat in baskets in the center of each table to be used during the tasting. She hadn't noticed those before. Only him.

"That's nice of your sister and her boyfriend to do," she said.

"Dakota volunteers at a local rescue, so there are always foster animals at the house. But we all agree that Zip is pretty darn cute."

Chantelle could say the same about York. He was better looking than she remembered.

"He just needs some socializing," he added.

Did York? He cleaned up nicely. Not that he'd looked bad last night.

"You're not wearing an apron," she said. "Are you off tonight?"

He nodded. "I'm not a regular employee. I'm filling in as needed. One employee is currently out of town and another is having a baby at the end of the month."

"Standing all day would be tiring if you're pregnant."

"Portia's been doing great up until now, but there's no reason for her to push herself too hard."

Curiosity got the best of Chantelle. "Portia?"

"She's the one having a baby. I'm taking over some of her shifts, so Dakota doesn't have to."

"You have time to do that?"

"I'm between jobs right now." His answer only raised more questions that were none of Chantelle's business. "I don't want Dakota to get too stressed. I'm here, so it makes sense to help out."

Something inside Chantelle melted a little. York Parker

seemed like a nice, thoughtful guy. Based on her dating experience, those were a rare breed, and her interest in him grew. "You're a good brother."

He shrugged. "I try to be."

She bet he succeeded more times than not. "Are you the oldest?"

"Yes. I'm four years older than Dakota."

His answer didn't surprise Chantelle.

"What about you?" he asked.

"I'm an only child."

"You get all the attention."

Got. Chantelle ignored the pang in her heart. She supposed that was one benefit, but she would have rather had siblings. Especially now that her dad was gone.

York waved at his sister, but the woman's forehead wrinkled when she saw Chantelle sitting with him. Protective of her brother or worried?

Chantelle almost laughed. No one had anything to worry about with her. All she wanted was to taste chocolate tonight. The more delicious it was, the happier she'd be.

He turned back to face her. "How do you like Marietta?"

"I haven't seen much of the town yet. Walking around is on tomorrow's agenda."

He cocked an eyebrow. "You have an agenda?"

If the shop's chocolates were tasty enough for her uncle to make a purchase offer, then yes, she had an agenda, but until she knew more... "More like a plan."

One that didn't include a good-looking guy who made her feel like she was a teenager with a crush. But she'd sat here and would stay put. That was the polite thing to do. She needed information about the shop and being rude would make her job harder.

"Anything in particular I should see?" she said.

"This is only my third day in town. When we were kids, we spent summer vacations here, so my favorites were the park and the movie theater. I'll ask my sisters for suggestions. Dakota has lived here a few years. Nevada's in town temporarily."

"Nevada and Dakota? Your sisters are named after states."

"So am I. My parents thankfully dropped the New from York."

"Geography buffs?"

"My mom and dad haven't told us why we were named after those states. Although, I have a pretty good idea."

The suggestive tone in his voice sent Chantelle's pulse racing. "Maybe they just like those states."

"Maybe." He didn't sound convinced.

"Not where you were born?"

"I was born in Montana. My dad was overseas at the time. My mom was staying with her aunt and uncle, who lived in Marietta."

"I'm sure your parents had their reasons."

He nodded. "What's it like being a chocolate expert?"

Chantelle pulled one of the tasting forms toward her. It seemed to have all the correct information. "Best job ever."

He laughed. "Can't beat that."

"You can't." She took a pencil and wrote her name on the sheet. No need to pull out her tablet. This would give her a place to take notes. "I travel all over the world, taste chocolate, and write about my experiences."

"Sounds like the perfect gig."

"It is." Gig described what she'd been doing these past three years. She couldn't wait to close this chapter in her life and move to France. She'd been doing what her uncle asked. At the same time, she'd built a solid reputation in the industry on her own. She would be an asset to Delacroix Chocolate.

An older gentleman walked to the table. "Looks like another sold-out event at the chocolate shop."

"I heard that's been happening lately," York said. "Walt Grayson, this is Chantelle Cummings."

"You wrote *The Chocolate Touch*." Walt's grin reached his eyes. "I'm sorry I missed your event last night, but I'm enjoying your book. Chocolate is the sixth food group. A necessity for human survival."

"Thank you," she said. "I like the way you think."

York smiled. "Walt is one of the regulars at Copper Mountain Chocolates."

Walt nodded. "One of many, though the staff makes us feel like we're all VIPs."

"Does the shop have a strong clientele year round?" she asked him.

"Yes," Walt said. "Business has only gotten better since the shop started these once-a-month special events like tonight's tasting."

Wanting to learn more from the man, she motioned to the empty chair across from her. "Why don't you join us?"

Walt stiffened, his smile fading. "I don't want to intrude."

"You're not," York said. "This is the table for those who came alone. Speaking of which, where's Bryce?"

The smile returned, and Walt sat. "At home."

"When there's chocolate to taste?" York asked.

Walt sighed. "Can you believe my son doesn't like chocolate?"

"I've heard those people exist," Chantelle joked. "But I've never actually met one."

"Well, if you come across Bryce Grayson while you're in town, that's him." Walt shook his head as if he couldn't understand his son. "On the flip side, his not liking chocolate means more for Dakota and me."

"Dakota and Walt's son are dating," York explained to Chantelle. "His son came to town when Walt broke both his legs last fall."

"I'm sorry that happened," Chantelle said. She could imagine that must have been a tough time. "You seem to be getting around well now."

"I am. Thanks." Walt's blue eyes twinkled. "I worked hard with my PT so I could be ready when Bryce and Dakota make things official."

"They will, but there's no rush." York glanced at his sister on the other side of the shop. "That's what my sister keeps saying, and I agree. Marriage can wait until Dakota's ready."

"Did someone say my name?" Dakota placed a plate filled with apple slices and bread on each table. "The tasting will be starting shortly."

Chantelle couldn't wait. She liked what she'd seen so far. The shop knew the importance of cleansing the palate between each piece being tasted. She hoped the chocolate didn't disappoint.

"Where's Rosie?" Walt asked Dakota.

"In Los Angeles with her brother," Dakota said. "She planned the trip so she could be back in town before Portia has the baby."

Chantelle had no idea who they were discussing, but she made a mental note. Rosie must be another member of the staff, along with Dakota and Portia. York was temporary help.

Now to see how Sage fit into all of this. Was she a hands-on owner? Was she a micro or macro manager? How committed was she to the chocolate shop?

"I'm going to get water for each of the tables so the event can begin." With that, Dakota walked toward the back of the shop.

"She works too hard," Walt said.

Nodding, York stared after his sister. "But Dakota's not doing as much as she used to. That's Bryce's influence. Now to get her to take a few days off."

"Good luck with that." Laughing, Walt picked up one of the forms and a pencil. He glanced at the paper. "They're going to make us work tonight."

"Your taste buds will be doing the work," Chantelle said. Tastings weren't always as social as some thought they'd be since distractions and conversations were kept to a minimum, but many people were surprised how much they learned when they focused on a piece of chocolate in their mouths. "You just have to write down what they tell you."

Walt wrote his name on his sheet. "I can do that."

"Me, too." York's gaze met hers and something fluttered in her stomach, a strange feeling that most likely had to do with the flecks of gold standing out among the greens and browns of his irises.

She stared transfixed, unable to look away, even though she should.

"Here comes Sage," Walt announced.

Chantelle blinked. Shifting her shoulders, she tore her gaze away from York. Probably best if she didn't glance his way again tonight.

Yeah, good luck with that.

Chapter Three

IGNORING THE VOICE in her head, Chantelle stared straight ahead. No problem. She didn't *have* to look at York. So what if he had a pretty face and equally stunning eyes? She could be professional. With her resolve firmly in place, she readied her pencil in case she wanted to jot down any notes.

A beautiful woman with long, red hair stood in front of the seated crowd. It had to be Sage. Chantelle had talked to her over the phone once. The chocolatier had extended an invitation to attend tonight's tasting.

"Good evening, everyone. I'm Sage Carrigan O'Dell." Her smile widened. "I'd like to welcome you to our tasting of Copper Mountain Chocolates."

People clapped. There seemed to be around twenty attending.

One person shouted, "Woo-hoo."

Chantelle studied the reactions. *Interesting*. Sage seemed to have quite the fan club in attendance.

"You'll notice we aren't playing music tonight. That's on

purpose," Sage continued. "It's important to concentrate and not be distracted by sounds and other things that can affect your senses."

Good. The chocolatier knew what she was talking about. Chantelle scooted forward in her chair. This little shop in the middle of nowhere Montana might be a hidden gem, but would its products shine bright enough for a spot in Delacroix Chocolates' recipe vault? She hoped so.

"The first thing we want to do is cleanse our palates." Sage raised a plate like the ones Dakota had passed out a few minutes ago. "You can use an apple slice or a cube of bread, and then follow that with a drink of water. Both steps are necessary, so don't skip either one. Let's get started."

Chantelle reached for a piece of bread. Her hand bumped York's. His skin was rough and warm. A shiver of awareness shot up her arm. *Uh-oh.* She fought the urge to jerk back her hand because her nerve endings quivered as if being awakened from a deep slumber.

What was going on?

She only knew the man's name, but that didn't stop the tingles from erupting in her stomach.

Forget butterflies.

This was a flock of seagulls.

Somehow, she managed to hold onto the bread and put the piece in her mouth. Not without effort and her full concentration. A good thing she needed to chew because that kept her from having to say anything. Not that she was a hundred percent sure she could find her voice.

As Walt bit into an apple slice, York leaned toward Chantelle. His warm breath sent more tingles shooting through her. Goose bumps prickled her skin.

The reaction to him made no sense. She tried to rationalize what was happening. York was good looking. Okay, he was gorgeous. Hot. But she wasn't looking for a fling. Those had never been her thing. She wanted to find true love, a lasting love.

Later.

Once she was back in the Delacroix fold so to speak.

"Ready to be impressed?" York asked.

His voice was deep and rumbled over her. If soundwaves had fingers, she'd be in big trouble.

She had no idea what he was talking about, but anticipation surged and her heart thudded.

Her gaze locked on his lips. Fuller than she realized, but would they be soft against hers? She met his eyes. Somehow…that wasn't much better than his mouth.

Chantelle swallowed. "By the chocolate or something else?"

The words hung in the air as if suspended in a cartoon-dialogue bubble. Immediately, she regretted saying them.

She was flirting. Why? She didn't flirt.

At least she hadn't in a while, ever since she'd decided that living closer to family was what she wanted and had put a plan in place to make that happen. Why start something that would end once she moved across the Atlantic?

Not that York wanted anything permanent from her, but something was sizzling between them. It was as if the air had become electrified.

He drew back slightly, though not as far as she would have liked for her peace of mind. His lopsided grin sent her pulse speeding up more.

"Chocolate," he answered.

Laughter lit his eyes, and she had the funny feeling York knew he was getting to her. Looking away would be the smartest thing she could do, but she couldn't…even though he left her feeling out of sorts and more than a little lost.

"But the something else has…*possibilities*," he added.

Her temperature spiraled. Heat flooded her cheeks.

She was not unaware of Walt sitting at the table with them, but the older man had gotten quiet. Too quiet.

Chantelle picked up her water and drank. Unfortunately, the liquid did nothing to cool her off. If anything, she wanted more. More to drink, more of York.

She bit back a sigh.

This evening was not turning out as she'd expected. She only hoped *he* wasn't working when she paid a daytime visit to the shop.

Talk about a distraction. She took another sip.

"Better save some of that for the tasting." Humor sounded in York's voice.

Chantelle lowered the glass. She'd die before she admitted he was right. York had seen her flustered at the bookstore, but she needed to remain professional and detached.

She stared down her nose. A silly gesture, but one she hoped would get her back in control of the situation and herself. "Thank you, but I know how much I need."

And what she needed.

It wasn't him.

York was too charming and good looking, but he was far from perfect. The man knew nothing about the one thing Chantelle loved most—chocolate. Maybe if she fixated on that flaw, she would get through the tasting unscathed.

Walt's gaze traveled from the tasting sheet to the two of them and back again, but he still didn't say a word. That didn't mean she couldn't get a glimpse of the gears clicking in his brain through his observant gaze.

York raised his glass to Chantelle. "You're the expert."

Yes, she was, but she remembered something her uncle had told her the first time they'd met. The words seemed appropriate now. "There's always more to learn about chocolate."

And if she kept letting York distract her, she might as well go back to the hotel.

Maybe Sage could teach Chantelle something new. It wouldn't be York. The guy couldn't tell a truffle from a milk-chocolate buttercream. He might be able to teach her about other things that had nothing to do with chocolate…and she was sure they'd be just as enjoyable.

Stop thinking about him.

"I have lots to learn," he said. "Maybe you could give me the inside scoop about chocolate, so I won't need as much on-the-job training."

She didn't know if he was joking or not, but she didn't want to find herself being reeled in like a trout and served for dinner. Best to be all business with him. "Let's see how much you get out of tonight."

No way would she volunteer for the task of teaching him. Chantelle wanted to put distance between them, not agree to see him again. As much as she wanted to be professional, it was if a switch had been flicked that made her aware of his every movement, including the blink of his eyes. No man should have such pretty eyelashes.

But York Parker wasn't the reason she was in Marietta.

She was here to find amazing chocolate recipes for her uncle to purchase. Anything else, including a hot guy filling in temporarily, would only get in the way of making her dreams come true. And she wanted that more than anything.

She needed to stay focused if she wanted Uncle Laurent to hire her. There would be time to fall in love and find her happily ever after…once she was living in France.

THE CHOCOLATE TASTING wasn't turning out as York expected. Oh, he enjoyed learning about cacao beans from Sage. Walt was a hoot, and getting to talk to him away from

Bryce and Dakota made it obvious the older man had a soft spot for the middle Parker sibling.

But York was struggling. Big time.

All because of Chantelle Cummings.

Who knew eating chocolate could be so...*sexy*?

Sexy as in not being able to take his eyes off her and enjoy the samples himself. Not that he minded.

Except he wanted to be the one feeding her chocolate. His fingers would lift the decadent treat to her mouth. His fingertips would brush against her soft lips as he placed the piece on her tongue...

A warning bell sounded in his head, but he felt helpless to stop it.

Watching her go through each of the tasting steps was a total turn-on. Her facial expressions as the chocolate warmed in her mouth made him wish he'd worn a T-shirt instead of a long-sleeved dress shirt. The shop was getting warm, especially with the playful images forming in his mind.

Do not go there.

The words kept sounding in his head.

He couldn't go there...could he?

Listening to Chantelle talk about chocolate told him how much she knew about the stuff. Even Walt had read her reviews of various chocolate shops around the world and asked her a multitude of questions about the subject. There wasn't one she couldn't answer.

Smart and sexy.

It didn't get much better than that.

York was tempted to ask her something, too—if she wanted to grab a drink afterward. But he couldn't think about putting a move on her. Whatever happened would be casual and temporary. A night of fun wasn't worth the possibility of messing up an opportunity for Sage's shop. He couldn't chance doing anything that could impact or hurt Dakota. Not everyone could keep business and pleasure separate, and he had no idea about Chantelle's views on this.

That meant no flirting or anything else with her.

Walt rubbed his palms together. "I can't wait to see what's next."

The guy loved chocolate, but his enthusiasm was contagious. "Me, either."

"Here's the last sample for the evening." Dakota passed out another piece to each of them. It looked darker than the others to York.

"What is it?" Walt asked.

"You'll soon find out." With that, she went to the next table.

"Have you enjoyed what you've tasted so far?" Sage asked as she stood in front of the tables.

A resounding *yes* rose from the crowd. A few clapped.

Walt whistled. That made York laugh. The man had to be Copper Mountain Chocolates' biggest fan.

Sage's smile brightened her face. "How did you like the last one?"

People shouted their observations. York wanted to hear what Chantelle had to say. She wrote a few more lines on her page, but she remained quiet.

"Excellent comments." Smiling, Sage held a bar of chocolate. "The final chocolate tonight is our top seller. The single-origin dark chocolate bar contains seventy-two-percent Criollo from Venezuela."

"My favorite," Walt said. "You'll love it."

Chantelle grinned. "This is the one I've been waiting for."

A ball of heat ignited in York's gut. Man, he hadn't felt this kind of pull toward a woman in a long time. Even the sound of her voice got him going. The urge to touch her—just a brush of his hand like before—was strong.

Maybe his sister would be up for swinging by Grey's Saloon on the way home. A beer and a game of pool might get his mind off the enticing chocolate expert.

Dakota refilled water glasses. Her smile hadn't wavered once. She loved working here, and she'd told him how much doing these monthly events meant to her.

He liked seeing his sister happy, and he had to admit Bryce was good for Dakota. They balanced each other well. Not quite as much opposites as Nevada and Dustin, but Bryce curbed Dakota's tendency to put everyone ahead of her own needs, and he also happened to be crazy in love with her.

York hadn't thought he'd like the guy, but he did. His

sister's choice in men had improved, and from what York had seen so far, Bryce was a keeper. Nevada agreed with him. Dakota, however, kept saying there was no rush. No rush was York's philosophy toward relationships.

"Now that you have your sample," Sage said. "Let's go through each of the tasting steps."

Sage had instructed them on the proper way to taste chocolate, and York picked up his piece to check the surface and color. As he wrote on his tasting sheet, his gaze strayed to Chantelle.

She held her sample at different angles. All she needed was one of those jeweler's loupes to magnify the chocolate. She studied the piece with a look that was half-scientist, half-lover.

The desire in her eyes hit him like a left jab.

Something in his stomach tightened.

York wanted a woman to look at him the way Chantelle looked at the chocolate.

He shook away the thought. Someday, maybe. Not now. *No rush, remember?*

After years following his dad's rules and then being in the air force, York was finally free. He would travel all over the country with his new job. He'd thought travel—or at least many assignments at different bases—would be part of his air force experience, but it hadn't turned out like that. Now he couldn't wait to live out of a suitcase, but no way did he want to be leaving a girlfriend, or worse, a wife and kids, behind the way the colonel had.

A relationship would tie York down. Make him come home—wherever that turned out to be—for all the wrong reasons. A serious relationship was the last thing on his mind.

There would be time for a family later.

Much later.

But he could still watch and enjoy Chantelle. He doubted she was tempting him on purpose. She seemed too focused on doing her job to notice how sexy she was and how it was affecting him.

Or anyone else.

Time for him to find his own focus.

York examined his sample again. No air bubbles or other blemishes. The bar had a nice sheen and color, too.

Chantelle raised the sample toward her nose.

She sniffed. A serene curve to her mouth followed.

Her lips looked so soft and sweet. Kissable.

Anticipation flared.

Not going to happen.

Too bad.

York forced his attention to the chocolate. He sniffed the sample. The delicious scent made him want to take a bite, but that would go against Sage's tasting procedure. He'd been raised to follow orders, whether someone was watching him or not.

Chantelle broke her piece in half.

Snap.

The sharp sound resonated through the shop. That spoke of the high quality. Others broke theirs. York did, too.

Chantelle placed half her sample in her mouth.

He did the same, setting the chocolate on his tongue so the piece could melt. Sage said this was the best way to experience all the subtle flavors. Chewing too soon could ruin the taste. She also recommended limiting the number of chews when a person got to that point.

Who knew there were so many rules to tasting chocolate vs. just eating a piece?

But as the chocolate melted, he realized Sage's steps worked. Flavors came alive in his mouth. Cinnamon. A nut. He couldn't tell what kind, though.

The changing tastes were subtle and interesting.

He wrote down his observations. Okay, scribbled. His handwriting sucked since he preferred typing on a keyboard.

He glanced at Chantelle.

Her eyes were closed. A smile was on her face. But her expression was more than mere satisfaction. She seemed to be experiencing some sort of Nirvana in her mouth.

He stared, transfixed. His pencil slipped from his fingers before clattering against the table. A hundred thoughts ran through his mind from—*what was she tasting that he'd missed* and *did she look like that when she was being kissed*?

Look away.

That was the right thing to do, but he couldn't.

Okay, he didn't want to.

Her eyes opened, and she reached for her pencil. "This last one was fabulous."

She crammed notes on her page. While most people jotted a line or two with each sample, she'd written all over her tasting sheet, front and back.

"Cinnamon and hazelnut, then caramel and banana," she said. "The dry finish was superb. I'm impressed."

That had to be good news for Sage and Copper Mountain Chocolates. Except York wished there were more for her to sample, so he could watch.

"This is my favorite." Walt looked at York. "How about you?"

"I prefer the lower-percentage chocolate." The ones that tasted best to him had more sugar. "I like mine a little sweeter."

"Sweet is good," Walt said.

Chantelle nodded. "Just not too sweet."

York wondered how she defined that. "Beats too bitter."

She studied the other half of the sample she'd snapped off.

He didn't know if she'd heard him or was ignoring him. "Ready for more?"

"Yes." Smiling, she raised the other piece as if to bring it closer to the overhead lighting. "I know what my next review will be on."

York remembered what Dakota had said at the

bookstore. That would be big publicity for the shop. He had no idea what Chantelle did for a living other than writing books. "Is writing reviews what you do when you're not working on a book?"

"Yes, and I also write articles. I have a monthly column in a food magazine, as well as my own blog. I occasionally freelance."

He was the one impressed now. "You should talk to Sage if you have any questions. She makes all the chocolate in the back."

"She and her staff makes it," Chantelle said.

Walt shook his head. "Just Sage."

"Dakota and Portia package products. Rosie helps out occasionally, but the staff mainly works the counter while Sage is in the back," York added.

Chantelle tilted her head. "That must be a lot of work for one person."

He shrugged. "Sage manages just fine."

"I think I will speak with her while I have the chance." Chantelle stood and started making her way to his sister's boss.

Walt watched her go before slyly asking, "Is there a special someone in your life?"

York almost laughed given what had happened last week in Fiji. He'd gone on the trip with his friend, Adam, who was going to make the military his career. Their goal for the vacation had been to have as much fun as possible with as many pretty ladies as they could.

He and Adam had also agreed not to exchange contact info with any women they met. Vacation romances had an expiration date. That was the biggest part of their appeal. They'd succeeded until their third day on the island when York had helped a pretty brunette from Seattle when she fell off her paddleboard. Kayla, a nurse, had thanked York before cozying up to Adam—as if he'd been her knight in wet swimming trunks.

Adam had been attracted to her, so York backed off like any good friend would. But if Kayla had liked him instead, would he have spent every single minute with her like Adam had? Would they be talking about a future after only a few days together?

York didn't think so, but he was happy for his friend. He only wished he hadn't lost his favorite wingman for the rest of the vacation. Still, he'd found various women to keep him company until it was time to leave the tropical paradise.

"Not in the market for a relationship with all the travel and work I'll be doing," York said with relief. Leaving the military, visiting his sisters, and starting a new career that meant traveling ninety percent of the time were endeavors best done on his own. "With so much going on, I'm happy being unattached."

Walt wagged his eyebrows. "Are you sure about that?

"Yes."

"But you like Chantelle."

York stiffened. "What?"

"I saw the way you looked at her during the tasting."

Busted. He'd thought he was being stealthy, but staring wasn't a crime. "She's pretty, but I know nothing about her."

"You know enough," Walt said in a matter-of-fact tone.

York wouldn't mind talking to her more, or maybe even kissing her, but he wasn't about to let a man who played matchmaker know that. He needed to put an end to this now. "I was watching her tasting technique."

"And thinking what *she* might taste like."

Heat rushed up his neck. "I—"

"It's fine," Walt interrupted with a laugh. "Dakota told me a few things about you. You've served your country well. Now it's time to have fun."

If only… "I had fun in Fiji."

"Have more fun in Marietta."

The older man's matchmaking efforts with Dakota and Bryce were well known. Walt's intentions were good. York appreciated how much the man cared about his sister, but their mom was harping enough on him about finding a girlfriend and settling down. He didn't need the residents of his sister's small town to do the same thing while he was here.

"You succeeded in bringing your son and my sister together," York said with a lighthearted tone. Butting into people's business was part of life in a place like Marietta, but he was only visiting. "How about you quit while you're ahead?"

A knowing gleam filled Walt's eyes. His smile widened. "Bryce and Dakota would say the same thing, but you and Chantelle look good together."

York glanced her way. Her face was animated as she spoke to Sage. He picked up his water glass. "Chantelle is only passing through town. Me, too."

"Then you'd better not waste any time."

"My sisters—"

"Are both head over heels in love with their boyfriends. They won't mind. In fact, they'd probably like to see you with someone."

Dakota and Nevada hated when their mom interfered, so they knew better than to do the same with him. York shrugged.

"Was that a maybe or a yes?" Walt's smile made him look like a canary-eating cat.

"I'm not sure."

"That's better than a straight no. Think about it. Her."

York forced himself not to look at Chantelle. He didn't need to give Walt any more evidence that he was attracted to the woman. "You don't give up."

"Losing my wife unexpectedly taught me life is too short not to go for it. Whatever that *it* may be. Mine happened to be Dakota's foster dog Scout and foster rat Pierre. Only *you* know what yours is or will be."

York knew his wasn't this woman. The timing and situation were both wrong despite the attraction.

Chantelle returned to the table. "Thanks for the company, gentlemen. I'm still on East Coast time and about to start yawning nonstop. I'm going to head back to the hotel."

"Alone?" York asked.

She gathered her paper, purse, and jacket. "Yes."

Not on his watch. He stood. "I'll walk with you."

A funny expression—a mix of confusion and surprise—was on her face. A look he knew well. Growing up with two younger sisters was like receiving a PhD in females.

"Excuse me?" she asked.

The two words were full of emotion. He regretted flirting with her because she probably saw this as some sort of come-on or proposition. It wasn't. His offer had nothing to do with how she looked eating chocolate. This was a better-safe-than-sorry issue.

"It's dark," he said. "You shouldn't walk alone."

"The hotel is only a couple of blocks away, and I did the same walk last night after the book signing." She sounded annoyed.

He was used to it. Over the years, his sisters had tried to fight him, too. They'd lost every time. The same way she would. "If I'd known you were walking, I wouldn't have let you leave on your own then."

"Listen to the good captain," Walt said.

"Former captain," York corrected.

Chantelle's eyebrows drew together. "Captain?"

Walt smiled. "York is fresh out of the air force. A real

American hero."

York rubbed his thumb over his fingertips. He didn't want anyone making more out of what he'd spent the past decade or so doing. "Former military, yes. Not a hero."

Chantelle's eyes widened. "That's why you're between jobs?"

He nodded, though her surprise made him wonder what she thought he was doing here. Sponging off his sisters, perhaps? "I'm taking the month off."

She started to say something but stopped herself.

"You said you're tired. Let York escort you to the hotel." Walt didn't miss a beat. He spoke in a fatherly tone. Firm, but caring. "I'll give Dakota a ride to her house, and everyone will get home safe and sound."

Chantelle shook her head. "I'm fine. York can walk his sister home."

"Thanks, Walt." York ignored what Chantelle had said. He grabbed his coat from the back of his chair. This wasn't up for discussion or negotiation. "I'd appreciate that."

He wasn't trying to be pushy or sexist. This was something he would do for any woman—one of his sisters or a stranger—because escorting Chantelle back to the hotel was the right thing—the safe thing—to do.

Even in a small town.

York motioned toward the door. "After you."

He wasn't doing this to spend more time with Chantelle, but he couldn't deny wanting a few more minutes in her company without anyone else around.

Chapter Four

OUTSIDE OF COPPER Mountain Chocolates, Chantelle glanced to her left where York walked on the side closest to the curb. Her father had always taken that side, saying it was what a gentleman did. What did that say about York? Or the way he'd shortened his stride to match hers? He moved like an athlete—fluid and confident with a touch of swagger.

She didn't know what to make of York Parker.

Hot, yes. Polite, too.

Old fashioned and over protective, most definitely.

Some might call him a jerk for going caveman.

She'd thought the word back inside the shop.

But now…

Chantelle didn't know whether to be charmed by York's chivalry or annoyed by him not waiting for or listening to her reply about walking her home. Granted, he didn't know her, so he wouldn't know that she was the last person who needed rescuing. She could take care of herself and had been for years. She didn't need an escort or a bodyguard.

She hadn't put on her jacket inside, so she shrugged on the first sleeve. York took the jacket and helped her put it on. His hand brushed her neck and sent a burst of chills down her spine. He pulled her hair out from underneath the collar.

Just a gentleman or more? She couldn't tell.

"Nice evening," he said. "Not too cold."

She glanced at him again. "Gorgeous."

So not smooth, but he was, so her mind going there wasn't a stretch. She'd better be more careful around him.

York smiled at her.

Chantelle's mouth went dry. Enough fun for one night. This had to stop. Now.

"The sky," she clarified. "The sky is gorgeous."

He looked up as if to see what she was talking about. Of course, she hadn't a clue. Damage control was needed. And self-control.

Think. Think. Think.

"There are so many stars," she said a moment too late, but maybe he hadn't noticed. She hoped so because she felt like the geeky freshman talking to the star quarterback and making a fool of herself doing it. "Millions of them. In the sky."

She was rambling. Something about York—someone she didn't know, Chantelle reminded herself—made her nervous. She could barely think straight around him.

He nodded. "Head a mile or so outside of Marietta, and you'll see more. Little white dots everywhere you look. Much better than where I lived in Maryland. Where are you from?"

"Boston."

"Lots of city lights there."

She nodded.

"You can see lots of stars when you fly."

The guy had to notice he was getting to her, but she appreciated him not calling her out on it. "I'll have to remember that. Must be nice."

His gaze rested on her. "Beautiful."

He was talking about the sky, not her. At least that was the safe thing to think. But that didn't stop a fresh round of goose bumps from covering her arms.

"You should check out the view while you're here," he added.

Was he going to offer to take her to see "the stars?" A weight pressed on her shoulders. She was attracted to him, but she much preferred to think his walking her home was an act of chivalry, not him wanting to hit on her. Chantelle didn't want to deal with that, so she'd better watch that she wasn't sending the wrong signals. She probably had.

York was handsome enough to be a player. He had that clean cut, All-American good looks down. His clothes weren't fancy, but they were nice and let her know a killer body waited underneath. Yes, he could be a player.

Although if that were the case, that would make Walt his wingman. No, the older man was too sweet to do that. Unless York worked alone...

"When I spent time here each summer, my great-uncle would take us a few miles outside town—to where you couldn't see the lights from Marietta," York said before she could say anything. "I'd never seen so many stars in my life. Made me want to be an astronaut someday, so I could be closer to those lights and planets."

A hint of wonder filled his voice that sent a rush of warmth followed by anticipation through her veins, but then he went quiet. No invitation to drive out of town came. She wasn't sure whether to breathe a sigh of relief or feel a tad disappointed. Not that she wanted him to make a move, but she wouldn't mind seeing stars like he described.

Or getting to know more about him.

His mentioning being an astronaut gave her an easy question to ask. "Were you a pilot in the air force?"

"No."

She waited for him to say more, but he didn't.

Their footsteps sounded on the pavement. The silence wasn't that uncomfortable. Okay, yes, it was.

Time to remedy that. "I would have expected more people to be out tonight."

"Most places are closed. Only the restaurants and bars stay open past nine."

"No wonder I'm tired." Her body was three hours ahead. "At least the muggers don't seem to be roaming the streets tonight."

"I've never heard of muggers in Marietta, but the bad

guys usually stay hidden so you can't see them until it's too late."

She couldn't tell by his tone if he were joking or serious, but this was better than talking about starry skies and getting goose bumps. "Is that what you learned in the air force?"

"Nah, TV."

That made her smile. "Crime-show addict?"

"Guilty as charged. You?"

"End of the world, paranormal, and zombie shows are more my fare."

His grin reached his eyes. The result was breathtaking and brought chills again.

"Wouldn't have expected that." His surprised tone matched his words. "Why those shows?"

She forced herself to breathe, but that was hard to do with his attention focused on her. Maybe a slow breath or two would put the brakes on her sprinting pulse and let her find her voice. She cleared her throat. "This might sound weird."

"Nothing wrong with weird."

"Watching those shows makes me appreciate my quiet life."

"Quiet sounds better than drama filled and being chased by the walking dead."

"For sure." Chantelle avoided drama. Easy to do when she was alone so much. "It's easier to put any troubles or problems into perspective when you're not being chased by zombies or fighting to survive the end of an utter devastation,"

"Now that's a good point." He looked ahead. "But we all face that. It's how we let them get to us, whether they are big or small problems, that's the real issue."

"Yes." But this subject had turned a little too personal for her liking. Time for a new one. "If you weren't a pilot, what did you do in the air force?"

"Computers."

"That could mean anything from entering data to flying drones to sitting in one of the underground bunkers waiting to launch missiles and end life as we know it."

He laughed. "You weren't kidding about the shows you watch."

York hadn't answered her question. She gave him a knowing smile. "Top-secret stuff, huh?"

"How long will you be in town?"

She wouldn't let him get away with changing the subject. "Not answering means you're saying yes to my question."

"Feel free to believe that if you'd like, but you'd be wrong."

"Would I?"

He inhaled. "Smells like rain."

She knew when to give up, but she had a feeling the former captain likely did something confidential or secret in his old position. "The weatherman on the radio said sunshine throughout the weekend, and there's not a cloud in the sky."

"My sisters said Dylan Morgan is wrong ninety percent of the time."

"Guess we'll find out." She wouldn't mind seeing York all wet. On second thought—

"You never answered my question about how long you're staying in town."

"A week or so." She had a return ticket, but she would stay longer if Uncle Laurent wanted her to. "I've never been to Montana before, so I wanted to make the most of my visit."

"It's a good place to vacation. I'm here until the end of the month." He pointed across the street. "There's your hotel."

"That was fast." She'd been so focused on talking to him that she hadn't realized they'd turned onto another street.

"Marietta isn't that big."

"Or dangerous."

He peered around her as if to see if anyone was around. "You never know when a zombie might strike."

She smiled. Okay, he was more charming than annoying. "Two of us might have a better chance of fending off an attack than one."

"Exactly."

As they stepped off the curb to cross Front Street, he touched the small of her back. The touch wasn't intimate; it was more protective.

Her heart beat faster.

Though maybe he was just used to acting like a big brother to all women.

Chantelle stepped onto the sidewalk in front of the hotel. She wasn't used to anyone looking out for her. She had to admit it felt…good. Even if she didn't know him.

She took a breath. "Thanks for walking me back."

"You're welcome." He stopped near the entrance, turning to face her.

If he were a player, this was where he would ask if she wanted to get a drink or offer to see her to her room or—

"Have fun checking out Marietta," he said. "Be sure to stop by the chocolate shop to get a cup of Sage's hot chocolate. Dakota calls it a chocolate lover's ambrosia. The samples at the book signing weren't big enough. You need a full glass to appreciate its goodness."

Her mouth watered. "I will."

"Well, goodnight."

What? That was all he was going to say?

"Bye." Chantelle forced the word from her dry throat.

He turned and walked away.

She half expected him to look back.

He didn't.

Guess he wasn't a player and was doing a nice deed. The way a big-brother type or a good guy would.

Her shoulders dropped.

Why was she so disappointed about that?

THE NEXT MORNING, York stood outside Copper Mountain Chocolates while Dakota unlocked the front door. This was his first day of on-the-job training, and he looked forward to spending time with his sister. Being surrounded by chocolate was a bonus.

When she opened the door, a bell jingled. "Ready?"

"Sure," he said. "This will be fun, especially if there's an employee discount."

Shaking her head, she stepped inside.

He followed, closing the door behind him.

York glanced down at his button-down shirt in an indigo-blue color and dark jeans. The same thing Dakota wore. "I just can't believe I'm dressed like my sister."

"I know, but Sage likes us to be in uniform." Dakota's pink cheeks suggested she wasn't totally comfortable with it, either. "I have a feeling Mom would be all over this. I think the last time we matched was that Christmas Eve when she bought us all matching pajamas to wear."

"Red-and-white striped long johns," they said at the same time and then laughed.

He shook his head. "Don't forget the matching caps."

"We looked like life-sized candy canes."

"Mine and Dad's had the back flaps that opened if we had to go to the bathroom."

A case of the giggles hit Dakota. "I'd forgotten about that."

Sunlight streamed in through the large front window. The shop looked different from last night. Some of the round tables had been removed, and two rectangular display tables had been brought in. No wonder York had arrived home before Dakota. She'd had work to do after everyone left. Though Walt had helped, she'd said.

The aroma of chocolate filled the air. York inhaled the delicious scent. "It smells like someone is already working."

"Sage always arrives first, and she leaves after lunch unless it's busy."

"Good to know there's backup."

Dakota removed her coat and motioned for him to follow her into the back area of the shop.

Sage stood by a silver vat of some sort. Her hair was pulled back from her face, and she wore an apron. "Welcome, York. I'm busy right now, so I'll let Dakota give you the tour and teach you what to do."

He had no idea what all the equipment in this back section did, but the kitchen area looked like a mini-chocolate factory. "Sounds good."

"When you arrive at the store, come back here." Dakota motioned to a row of cubbies against a wall that were next to a rack of copper aprons. "You can leave your personal items in one of these. That includes your cell phone. Clock in here." She showed him where to punch his time card. "And remember to put on a clean apron."

York removed his wallet and cell phone, placing them in

a cubby. A time card with his name on it was waiting for him. Not surprising since Sage seemed like the organized type.

He punched in. Next came the apron, like the one he'd worn the other night.

"Now what?" he asked.

"A quick tour, and I need to show you where the supplies are kept."

The shop was small, so it didn't take long.

As he joined Dakota behind the glass display counter, he noticed a copper pot of hot chocolate simmering on a countertop burner. That must be why the shop smelled so good. No wonder Dakota liked working here. The aroma couldn't be beat.

After a lesson on the cash register and credit-card machine, he practiced swirling a tower of whipped cream on a mug—though his cup was full of water instead of hot chocolate—and how to greet customers as they walked in the door.

"Let's try it," Dakota said. "Jingle, jingle, jingle."

"Welcome to Copper Mountain Chocolates," he replied.

"Good, but be sure to smile."

He tried again. "Welcome to Copper Mountain Chocolates."

"Better. Again."

He continued until Dakota was satisfied. "Never knew you were such a taskmaster."

"I'm not, but Sage has high standards."

The implication was clear to York. His sister didn't want him to mess up. He wouldn't let her down.

"All this seems easy enough." The change from being underground in an air-conditioned room with monitors and computers was welcome. He looked forward to interacting with people, too. That hadn't happened in his old job unless talking to coworkers counted. "What do I do if there aren't customers? Stand here and look pretty?"

"Ha-ha." Dakota pulled out a three-ring binder from beneath the counter. "There's a list in here. If Sage has anything special for us to do, such as price markdowns or packaging items, she'll add a note. There's usually a table to clear, and you can always clean if there's nothing else to do."

"Now you sound like Mom."

"Please don't say that."

"It's true."

Dakota stuck out her tongue.

"There's also a list of the chocolate that will be the daily sample." She put on gloves, pulled out a white plate, and removed chocolates from the display counter. "Today's is the dark chocolate hazelnut bark. Put out a few pieces so they're ready and add to it as needed. And these are samples for the *customers*."

The way she emphasized the last word made him laugh. "No eating while on duty. I'm familiar with that rule."

"You'll do fine." Her smile widened. "Just remember,

some customers will be talkative, but others want to get in and out with saying as little as possible."

"I'll pay attention to how customers come across. I get along with most people."

"You and Chantelle Cummings seemed to hit it off last night."

No way did he want to have this discussion with his sister. He shrugged even though he'd been thinking about Chantelle since last night. "Forced proximity."

"According to Walt—"

"You mean Mr. Wannabe Matchmaker?"

Dakota laughed. "You're right, but you were checking her out."

"Looking never hurt anyone."

"Attracted to her?" Dakota asked.

"She's pretty, but no," he said quickly. "And even if I were, give me some credit, sis. No matter how I felt about her, I wouldn't hit on a woman who is writing a review of your boss's chocolate."

Dakota's lips parted. "A review? Really?"

"Chantelle mentioned that last night."

His sister rubbed her hands together. "A review would be fantastic. Did she say anything about coming by the shop today?"

"No." And York hoped she didn't. He wanted to focus on his new job and not be distracted. Speaking of which, he glanced at the clock. "It's ten."

Dakota walked to the front door, unlocked it, and flipped the sign from closed to open. "Remember, no tasting the sweets during work hours." A mischievous gleam filled her eyes. "That includes chocolates and pretty customers."

He shook his head. "After work hours?"

Dakota winked. "Help yourself."

Uh-oh. She was becoming as bad as Mom.

Chapter Five

THE TIME PASSED quickly.

Customers came in and out, some for a sample and others to purchase chocolate. York struggled to keep up.

Dakota helped him, as did Portia when she showed up later, but he still got things mixed up. He gave one person the wrong piece of chocolate. He'd forgotten to offer a sample to another. He couldn't remember the name of the dark-haired girl who Dakota said came in every week day around lunchtime to write or sketch and worked for the shop's marketing firm. And he couldn't quite get the knack of tying a neat bow on a bag. His fingers just weren't that good at tying ribbon.

Portia, who had been working at the shop since October, kindly assured him those types of mistakes were normal and reminded him the young woman's name was Gretchen Zabrinski.

Maybe, but he wasn't used to feeling so…incompetent.

He was used to computer keyboards, not a cash register. Who knew customer service with a smile could be so…challenging? Thankfully, things slowed after lunchtime.

A customer sat at one of the tables as he waited for his hot chocolate. The guy looked like a cowboy with jeans, boots, and a hat on an empty chair.

York carried over the mug and a small napkin.

If only the guys at the base could see him now…

A good thing they couldn't because they would be laughing their butts off.

With care, he set the drink in front of the man. Nothing spilled.

Progress. "Here you go."

"Thanks." The man looked at him. "Filling in for Rosie while she's away?"

York nodded. The customer must be a regular. There seemed to be a lot of those given this wasn't the first time he'd heard the question. "I'm Dakota's brother. Let me know if you need anything else."

As York returned to the counter, Portia came out of the back with a restocked plate of the day's sample.

"Hey, Eli," Portia said.

The cowboy studied her. "Looks like you're ready to pop."

Somehow, Portia kept a smile on her face. Yes, she looked as if she had tucked a beach ball under her shirt. The apron didn't quite fit due to her large pregnant belly, but unlike Eli, York knew better than to say that aloud.

She blew out a breath. "You sure have a way with

words."

Eli grinned. "That's what all the ladies tell me."

"Oh, the mama cows talk to you?" Portia winked.

Eli laughed and raised his glass to her. "I probably deserved that."

Not probably, York thought.

"When are you due?" Eli asked in between sips of his cocoa.

"End of the month." Portia joined York behind the counter. "Here's more of the dark chocolate bark. Dakota's washing dishes. Sage left early to go to Savannah's school, and she told me to tell you that you did a good job today."

Pride filled him. Selling chocolates was about as far away from what he normally did as possible, but he'd had fun. It wasn't just spending time with Dakota; he also liked talking to the people who came into the store.

He took the tray from Portia and placed it on the counter near the cash register. "Thanks."

Portia rubbed her lower back.

"You okay?" he asked her.

"I'm not sleeping much. I think this baby is going to be a gymnast or a soccer player. Since you and Dakota are here, I'm probably going to cut out early."

"Leave whenever you want. Dakota's in the back, and I'm here so you don't have to be."

York knew nothing about pregnancy or babies, but being young, single, and expecting a baby had to be rough. Both his sisters were worried about Portia, and he understood their concern. No one knew if she was planning to keep the baby or not. Dakota said a young man with a bouquet of flowers had been by the shop once to visit Portia, and flowers had arrived on Valentine's Day, but she still hadn't mentioned who the father was to anyone.

Portia didn't have a big brother, and York would gladly be a surrogate if she needed one. He walked to the closest table and pulled out a chair.

"You're tired. Sit for a few minutes before you go." He tilted his head toward their one customer who was drinking hot chocolate. "It's quiet in here. I can hold down the fort for a few minutes or ask for help if I need it."

Portia slowly lowered herself into a chair. "Thanks."

As York stepped behind the counter, the bell on the door jingled. "Welcome to Copper Mountain Chocolates."

"Hello," a woman said.

Not just any female voice. One he recognized from last night. He needed to concentrate on doing his job and not let her distract him. "Hi, Chantelle."

Greeting customers was part of his job.

As she walked toward the counter, Eli checked her out from behind. Not that York blamed the cowboy. He imagined that view was nice given the sway of her hips, but York's view of her front was great, too.

Her skirt swooshed above her knees and made her legs look long, even with slip-on flats. No heels required. She had a jacket tucked over her purse, which hung from her shoulder. Her short-sleeved shirt showed off pale but toned arms.

She looked at the chocolates in the display case. "I thought I'd stop by to see what the place looks like in the daylight and try a hot chocolate."

"Welcome." York realized he'd already said that, so he picked up the plate of samples. "I'll make you a cup. Would you like to try our dark chocolate hazelnut bark in the meanwhile?"

"I'd love a piece."

He managed to hand her the sample on a napkin without dropping anything. York didn't know why her arrival brought a sudden rush of anxiety. Maybe because he wasn't expecting her to show up.

Or look so good.

She raised the chocolate to her glossed lips.

Look away.

York should, but like a moth about to dive bomb a lit candle, he couldn't. Truth was he didn't want to. Something about the way she ate chocolate drew him in.

Okay, turned him on.

As if she could read his mind, Chantelle faced away from him. "The shop looks different. Last night's table arrangement isn't typical?"

"I—" He looked at Portia. "This is Chantelle Cummings. She wrote *The Chocolate Touch*."

Portia's lips parted. She used the table to push herself up.

Her movements were slow and awkward, but she was soon standing.

"Hi, I'm Portia." She shook Chantelle's hand. "I've enjoyed reading your articles on chocolate."

"Thanks."

Grateful Portia was there to answer questions, York went to work on Chantelle's hot chocolate. He pulled a white mug off the shelf.

Stirring the hot chocolate simmering in the pot, he pictured the most perfect cup of cocoa possible.

That was what he wanted to make Chantelle.

And not just because he wanted to show off his new skills for the attractive woman with the chocolate touch. Well, maybe he did a little. But he also knew her visit was important to the shop itself.

He spooned the creamy mixture into the cup. Carefully, with the steady hand that would be the envy of hot-chocolate makers everywhere, he added a swirl of whipped cream the way Dakota had taught him earlier today. She'd been right that it got easier each time.

Portia started talking to Chantelle. "You wanted to know about the table arrangement. During our monthly events, we move out everything that isn't bolted down. We then bring in additional tables and chairs based on what we're doing and how many tickets we've sold. Sage hired a marketing person, Krista Martin, in December. So far, most of the events she planned have sold out. Our Valentine one lasted for days, so we had to work around the extra tables that were needed for the competitors to use."

York sprinkled shaved chocolate over the whipped cream. He could only see Chantelle's back, but he'd been correct about that view.

Stop leering.

"Competitors? What kind of events do you hold here?" Chantelle asked.

"Wine tasting and chocolate pairings. Truffle making. June will be a series of speed-dating events. During February, we teamed up with a local wine shop and feed store to sponsor The Valentine Quest, which was an adventure-type race. York just got back from his vacation in Fiji, which was the grand prize."

"You participated?" Chantelle asked.

"No. I was in Maryland when this happened. I was just the lucky recipient of the grand prize thanks to my younger sister's boyfriend Dustin."

She gave him the once-over. "That explains your tan."

Nothing in the way she said the words told him if that was a compliment or not.

Chantelle's gaze scanned the shop again. "Is this your typical retail setup?"

"Yes. The decorations change each month." Portia took a step toward one of the tables that displayed boxes of chocolate, but then she doubled over in what looked like pain. "Oh."

York ran to Portia.

Eli was at her side in an instant, too.

Dakota rushed out of the back. "What was…Portia?"

Fear filled the young woman's eyes. Portia grimaced. "I…"

York and Eli helped her back into the chair.

"Is it the baby?" York asked, feeling way out of his element here.

Chantelle's face was pale. She held onto her cell phone. "Should I call 911?"

Portia shook her head. "No, it can't be the baby."

"Rachel Vaughn had her baby a little early, and everything turned out just fine." Eli kneeled next to Portia. His voice was full of confidence, and York envied the cowboy's coolness. "My older sister had false labor for days. The hospital kept sending her home each time she went in to be checked out."

Dakota's gaze hadn't left Portia. "Why don't we go to the hospital? They can tell you what's going on."

Portia shook her head. "It's too soon. I'm not…ready."

"That's okay. Let's go anyway." Dakota's voice was calm and her tone light. York had never been prouder of his sister. He knew by the way she kept flexing her fingers that she was trying not to freak out, but she didn't let Portia see it. "After you're released, we can have a good laugh and go out to dinner. You can add this to your baby-book memories."

"Sounds like a good plan," Eli said before Portia could

answer. "I've got my truck parked right outside. I can drive you there."

York nodded. "I agree."

"Me, too," Chantelle chimed in.

"Everything will be okay." Dakota held Portia's hand. "Eli will drive, and I'll go with you, too. We can call your aunt and mother on the way, okay?"

Portia pressed her lips together. Her eyes darkened with a mix of fear and nerves that made York want to do something—anything—to bring back his sister and the young woman's smiles.

"Could we wait to find out what's going on before we call anyone?" Portia asked.

Dakota smiled. "Of course."

"What can I do?" York asked.

"Stay here," Dakota said. "I'll call you once I know more. I know this is your first day, but—"

"Go." He knew Portia needed people she knew with her. Of the four people in the shop, that was Dakota and Eli. "I can muddle my way through if I don't know something."

Chantelle took a step forward. "I can stick around if that would help. I don't know how you run things here, but I know chocolate."

Relief flashed across Dakota's face. "That would be great. Thanks."

"I'll get your stuff." York bolted into the back and grabbed everything out of their cubbies. That included purses, jackets, and phones. He ran back into the store area and handed them over to Dakota. "Here you go."

Eli was helping Portia to her feet. "I can carry you."

"It's not that far," Portia said. "I'd rather walk."

"Then let's go." Eli seemed to be in a hurry.

That worried York because the cowboy was the only one who had experience with pregnant women. Did Eli know something everyone else didn't?

Portia took a step while Eli supported her.

"Everything will be fine," the cowboy said.

"Fine," Portia repeated.

The bell jingled when Dakota opened the door for them, and as quickly as the excitement began, it was over. The shop was quiet, and York was there with Chantelle.

Alone.

She blew out a breath. "Wow. Never had that happen at a chocolate shop before."

"I've never had that happen anywhere before." Not even on base with coworkers who had been pregnant. A heavy weight pressed down on him. He glanced out the front window to see Eli's pickup driving off. "I hope Portia's okay."

"She seems very nice."

Today was the first time York had met her, but... "She is."

If he stood here doing nothing, he was going to go crazy. He looked around the shop, spotting a cup and a crumpled-up napkin on one of the tables. He made a beeline to where Eli had sat and cleaned the area. Now York had to find a few more things to do.

Although he was concerned about Portia and her baby, he was also worried about being alone with Chantelle. He had a feeling he would screw up if he tried to talk to her again because all he could think about was where he wanted to take her for dinner…and dessert.

STANDING NEXT TO the display case, Chantelle watched York clear the table without a wasted motion or word. He seemed…stressed. Not only that, but he scrubbed as if a contagion on the tabletop could wipe out mankind if he didn't eradicate it first.

Worried, trying to keep busy, or a combination of the two?

She understood why he needed to keep himself busy because she couldn't stop thinking about Portia, either. Chantelle hoped the young woman and her baby were okay. Like York, Chantelle needed to do something other than stand here.

"York," she said finally.

He stopped wiping and glanced her way. He seemed to have forgotten she was there. "Chantelle. Sorry. I…wasn't expecting this to happen. Dakota seemed worried, Portia looked scared, and I'm not sure what I should be doing."

His honest words matched how Chantelle was feeling. The urge to reach out to him was strong, but the distance between them kept her from doing that. "Same here."

"It's my first day."

"One you won't forget."

"That's for sure."

His smile returned full force and hit her like an unexpected gale. She took a step back. Swallowed. Might have been better for her if he continued to be wigged out, but she really liked that smile of his.

"I'm happy you're here," he added.

"Me, too." And she was. Because of him.

Helping was something her parents had taught her to do. She'd grown up being taught the importance of lending a hand if she could. Yet, more was at play here. York Parker intrigued her, even if she knew better than to feel that way.

And she did know better.

But some things—like a second piece of chocolate—weren't that bad for a person. She hoped that was the case with York.

"Should I put on an apron and stand behind the counter?" she asked.

"Oh, yeah. That would be good."

He wiped the table again. If he kept that up, his next job would be to refinish the wood.

"Where are the aprons?" she asked.

He straightened. "In the back. Sorry. I keep thinking

about…"

"Me, too."

His gaze met hers, and he straightened. "There are clean aprons hanging by the cubbies. You can leave your purse and jacket inside one of them."

"Will do."

"The restroom is back there, too. Wouldn't want you to have to wander around to find it."

The amusement in his voice reminded her of two nights ago. He'd remembered what had happened at the bookstore. She hadn't forgotten one second of their encounter.

She walked toward a door she assumed led to the back as it was where Sage and Dakota had disappeared into during the tasting last night.

Chantelle stepped into a small chocolate factory complete with an industrial-grade stove and roaster.

This was where the magic happened…

A rush of excitement flowed through her.

When she was younger, her mother had told her chocolate makers were magicians who used magic to create the most wonderful things to eat. After touring the Delacroix chocolate laboratory in Bayonne with her uncle, she knew her mother was correct. Seeing all the people working together, and the traditions created by her grandfather, had made the factory feel like home and the employees extended family.

Definitely magic.

But it wasn't as simple as waving a magic wand, saying abracadabra, and pulling a piece of chocolate out of a hat. Each chocolatier had their own process, but the steps were similar. Cacao beans had to be roasted, cracked, and the nibs heated to remove the husk. But those were only a few of the steps. The process took days for chocolatiers like Sage to complete, but the results were worth the time and effort.

Quality over quantity.

The smells were sharper than out in the retail section. No doubt because the ingredients were stored here.

Inhaling, Chantelle captured the scents of cinnamon and vanilla bean. A hint of chili powder, too.

A potpourri of chocolatey goodness.

Excitement shot to her fingertips.

Her dad had once joked that chocolate ran through Delacroix veins. That seemed to be the case with her mother and uncle. Would it be true for her and her cousin?

The cubbies York had mentioned were against a wall. She placed her jacket and purse inside one. A wallet and phone filled another. It had to be York's stuff. The rest were empty. As he'd said, the aprons were hanging right there, so she grabbed one.

After another glance around the mini-factory, she grinned. A satisfied feeling settled over her. The urge to take a photo or two for her report was strong, but she couldn't without permission. Chocolatiers guarded their processes and recipes like state secrets.

Nothing in Chantelle's reports would be considered confidential. Much of her research was done online prior to her visit. She then formed opinions based on what she saw, tasted, and the answers given to her questions. Once she decided, she gave a buy-or-pass recommendation to her uncle.

Still, she couldn't believe her luck. Not only did she get to see a different side of Copper Mountain Chocolates, but she also had the chance to view the retail side of a chocolate shop from the other side of the counter. Getting customer-service experience was one of the steps on her uncle's list.

She couldn't wait. One afternoon helping in a shop wouldn't count as enough experience, but it was a start.

After she tied the apron strings behind her back, she walked out to the front.

York stirred a copper pot on the burner. "Your hot chocolate is cold."

Chantelle had forgotten about it. "No problem. I'm sure there are rules about eating and drinking while working."

"There are. You're welcome to keep a drink or water bottle in your cubby for when you get thirsty."

"I'm fine, and hot chocolate isn't something to leave sitting out like that. I'll come back tomorrow for another."

He looked over his shoulder at her, a corner of his mouth turning up higher than the other in a charmingly lopsided grin. "On me for helping out today."

That must mean he planned to be here tomorrow.

"Sounds good."

He set the spoon on a holder and faced her. "Least I can do for you. The selling part hasn't been difficult, other than figuring out how to do more than a couple of things at once, but I don't know enough about chocolate to answer questions. Some customers are total foodies."

"Or chocolate lovers."

People passed in front of the large window that contained a springtime chocolate display, but no one was slowing down or stopping. That meant the shop might stay empty for a few more minutes.

"No one's in here, so stand in front of the case like a customer would and study the labels. I'll quiz you later," she suggested.

"Is that how you learned?"

"I learned the names of chocolates by making them with my mother, but this will work in a pinch."

"Your mother makes chocolates?"

"She did." Chantelle felt a pang, but not as intense as it had once been. "She died. It was a long time ago."

He touched her shoulder. "I'm sorry."

His hand was large. Heat flowed through the fabric of her shirt to the skin below. That was unexpected.

"Thanks." There wasn't anything else she could say.

He lowered his arm, and she immediately missed his warmth. She wasn't used to comforting touches. She missed that. Hugs, too.

She picked up the spoon from the holder. "I'll stir the hot chocolate. If a customer enters, come back here as fast as you can."

He looked like he wanted to laugh.

"What?" she asked.

He studied her, but she had no idea why. "Nothing."

"Start memorizing."

"Will do." He walked around the counter. "Almost forgot. If you hear the bell jingle, say…"

"Welcome to Copper Mountain Chocolates," Chantelle replied with her brightest smile. "This isn't my first time at the rodeo, cowboy."

"No, it's your second." Gratitude filled his eyes. "Thanks for sticking around to help me today. This store's customers deserve better than me."

The sincerity in his voice made her heart bump.

Not only was he attractive, but he was also sweet and responsible.

Questions formed in her mind, but she couldn't ask him anything personal no matter how much she wanted to know the answer.

Be professional.

That would be expected of her at Delacroix Chocolates. Being at Copper Mountain Chocolates today was no different. She couldn't embarrass herself by letting a handsome face and killer body get to her again.

She pushed back her shoulders. "I don't see you studying

yet."

"You're as bad as my sisters."

"I'll take that as a compliment."

Hot chocolate simmered in a copper pot. The scents of vanilla and cinnamon rose from the mixture. She couldn't wait to taste a full cup tomorrow.

The bell on the door jingled.

"Welcome to…" The words *Delacroix Chocolates* almost came out, but she swallowed them back. "Copper Mountain Chocolates."

York hurried to her side of the counter. He wiped his hands on the front of his apron, and then did it again.

Sweaty palms? Even if not, Chantelle thought the action was cute.

A tall, elegant blonde dressed in a thigh-length sweater, which was belted at the hips, leggings, and knee-high boots closed the door behind her.

Maybe York was nervous for another reason. A funny feeling settled in the pit of Chantelle's stomach. She had no right to be bothered by the thought of him with someone else, but she kind of was.

What was up with that?

The customer looked over at the display counter. Her gaze narrowed. "Who are you two?"

The woman's tone wasn't rude. It was more surprised, but the question startled Chantelle. She had visited chocolate shops, never worked in one, but maybe customers didn't worry about filters when they spoke to cashiers.

"I'm York Parker, Dakota's brother."

The woman's glossed lips formed a perfect O.

"This is Chantelle. We're helping out today." York put on a plastic glove, picked up a pair of silver tongs, and raised a white plate full of chocolate. "Would you like to try today's sample? It's dark chocolate hazelnut bark."

The woman hesitated.

"It's fresh. Sage made the batch this morning," he added.

"Sure." That seemed to sway the woman. "I'll have a piece."

As she took her sample, Chantelle noticed the woman's smooth skin and nicely manicured nails. The pink pearly polish was perfect for a hand model.

"I'd also like a Criollo bar, two chocolate buttercreams, and three champagne truffles," the woman said.

"I'll get those for you." Chantelle picked up a small box and glanced at York, who nodded.

Interesting. They made a good team. At least with this first customer.

Chantelle filled the box with the selected chocolates.

"I'm DeeDee Cash. I've been back in Marietta since last month, but I haven't seen either of you around."

"Nice to meet you, DeeDee. I'm staying with my sisters for a few weeks." York rang up the order. "Chantelle is passing through town, but the shop wanted to take advantage of her chocolate expertise today."

Very smooth, Mr. Parker. Chantelle smiled at him and the customer.

"Where is everyone else?" DeeDee asked.

"They're out right now." Without missing a beat, York told DeeDee the amount she owed and took her credit card. "If you'd like another sample, we won't tell."

The guy might not know chocolate, but he was a pro at talking to customers. Not everyone had that gift. Chantelle was impressed.

"No, but thanks. What I bought will be more than enough," DeeDee said.

Chantelle closed the box and placed it inside a bag. She noticed the spool of ribbon and a pair of scissors, so she cut off a piece and tied a bow around the bag's handles. That was what Delacroix Chocolates and most other shops she'd visited did, so she assumed that was why the ribbon was there.

She handed the bag to DeeDee. "Enjoy your chocolates."

As soon as the woman left the shop, York blew out a breath. "I had no idea how to answer her question about the rest of the staff. Dakota warned me that many people in town are nosy, so I didn't feel right mentioning Portia in case her family doesn't know she's at the hospital yet."

Chantelle patted his arm. The muscles were firm beneath her fingers. She remembered that from when she'd stumbled into him. "You did well. DeeDee didn't question it at all."

"Good. Thanks."

His charming smile sent tingles shooting all the way to Chantelle's toes. The reason, however, made her feel childish. He hadn't smiled like that at DeeDee.

He pointed to the ribbon. "You're in charge of bow tying. I'm all thumbs."

"My hands are smaller." Speaking of which, hers was still on his arm. She pulled her arm to her side. "And I have more experience."

"Not only are you an expert on chocolate, but also you tie bows."

"Something like that."

"Well, your bows look great. Mine are nothing but tangled ribbon."

She wouldn't mind tangling her fingers in his hair to see if it was soft. On second thought, bad idea.

She stepped away from him. "How's the studying going?"

"I've got the salted caramels down."

"Caramels, huh?" She knew the sea salt and shape were dead giveaways, but... "Isn't that the one you knew at the book signing?"

He bit his lower lip. "Yes."

York's mouth slanted in the most adorable expression. One more geeky than hot. All he needed were thick plastic glasses to complete the image.

She loved the unexpected change. Still attractive, but he looked more like a nerdy computer guy now instead of some hunky, action-hero type. Approachable, not trouble to avoid.

She pointed to the chocolates in the display case. "What are you waiting for?"

"Oh, right. Better get memorizing. Especially if there's going to be a quiz."

"Don't worry, I'll go easy on you. Learn the bottom row of chocolates today and the top row tomorrow."

He winked. "You want another reason to come back tomorrow."

Heat rushed up her neck because that was exactly what she wanted. She breathed in as if that could stop the flush from reaching her face.

"The hot chocolate is so good you don't need an excuse to drop by," he added.

Relief made her tense shoulders loosen. She'd forgotten all about the hot chocolate. "Good to know."

Except he was the reason she wanted to come back. Yes, he was good looking and she couldn't calm the butterflies in her stomach when he was around, but he also made her smile. Something she didn't do much of these days when she was alone. She was too focused on impressing Uncle Laurent. Fun had taken a backseat to her pseudo-apprenticeship.

The bell on the door jingled.

"Welcome to Copper Mountain Chocolates," York said before she could. As he joined her behind the counter, he winked.

Their new customer—an older woman—peered at the

chocolates. She looked up. "You two are new."

York nodded. "First day for us both."

First and last day for Chantelle, but she kept quiet. She was helping, not working like York. He might be a newbie and not one-hundred-percent confident in his new position, but he could handle this.

"Would you like a sample?" York raised the plate.

"No, thank you. I'm not a fan of nuts." The woman motioned to the glass display. "But I would like two dark chocolate salted caramels."

"Those are one of my favorites."

"Mine, too," the woman said. "We have excellent taste."

"Yes, we do." He glanced at Chantelle.

I've got this. She could tell he was thinking that, and his confidence made him more attractive.

Still, she had one word for him.

Show-off.

He put on plastic gloves. "I like how the taste of salt mixes with the caramel and chocolate. Nothing quite like that flavor combination."

"So do I," the woman agreed.

York used tongs to pick up two caramels and place them into a bag. "Would you care for anything else?"

The woman's green eyes danced. She tucked a white curl behind her ear. If she were any younger, Chantelle would think the move was flirtatious.

"Not unless you'd like to go out with my granddaughter," the woman said with a grin. "She's been wanting to find a nice young man."

York's face turned tomato red. Chantelle had no doubt if his hair wasn't covering the tips of his ears, she could see that those were red, too.

"I'm, uh…" Whatever he wanted to say wasn't happening.

Poor guy. The least Chantelle could do was help him out the way he'd assisted her at the bookstore.

"York is a very nice man," she said. "But unfortunately, he's only here for a few weeks. He has a jam-packed schedule between family obligations and his work schedule."

He nodded like those bobble-head dolls they gave away at baseball games at Fenway Park.

She may have earned herself a second free cup of hot chocolate with this save.

The woman tsked. "That's too bad. But you're more my type than hers, anyway. Well, my type fifty years ago."

Her pleasant laugh didn't stop York's blush from returning deeper than before.

Chantelle bit back a giggle. She wondered what the woman's granddaughter would think about that tidbit of information.

The customer paid for her caramels and then headed to the door. Before stepping outside, she glanced back and gave York a blatant once-over with zero hesitation or embarrassment.

As soon as the door slammed, Chantelle burst out laughing. "Oh, boy. You are going to be as popular as the chocolates and have your own fan club soon."

He shook his head. "The lady was just being nice."

"That wasn't quite naughty, but I wouldn't call what she did nice."

York waved his hand as if he could make what happened go away.

Chantelle liked seeing him flustered. "I bet this is only the beginning. You should find out if there are rules about dating customers."

His gaze met hers. "I'd rather find out if there are rules about going out with coworkers."

"Coworkers?" Her voice cracked. Had he meant her?

An intense look in his eyes, he took a step closer.

The bell jingled, and the two jumped away from each other. Chantelle wasn't sure if he said the greeting or she did, but that started a steady stream of customers into the shop for the next two hours.

The entire time, Chantelle couldn't stop thinking about what York had said.

I'd rather find out if there are rules about going out with coworkers.

Was he planning to ask her out?

And if he did, what should she say?

Yes?

No?

Maybe?

Part of her hoped York was joking. She didn't want to listen to what the other part of her wanted. A good thing she was only working with him this afternoon…or who knew what might happen?

Chapter Six

YORK DIDN'T MIND having a shop full of customers. Keeping busy with orders was better than being alone with Chantelle, especially when he'd almost asked her out. That would have been a stupid move.

"How can I help you?" he asked a young girl and her mother.

The girl, who was around ten or so, placed a copper box filled with chocolates on the counter. "This, please."

He rang up the order. "Is it a gift?"

"Yes, for my teacher."

"In that case, I'll have our bow master make this look even prettier for you." He handed the box to Chantelle, who went right to work as he took payment from the girl's mother.

Chantelle handed over a bag that was filled with tissue paper and tied with a pretty bow.

The girl's grin reached her eyes as she bounced on her toes. "Thank you."

Chantelle curtsied. "My pleasure."

No doubt spending time outside the chocolate shop with Chantelle would be a pleasure.

He swallowed a sigh.

In his defense, wanting to go out with Chantelle wasn't a completely random idea. They were both in town for a brief time, and they had fun working together. At least he was.

He enjoyed spending time with her.

Who wouldn't?

Chantelle's smile brightened her face like the sun appearing over the horizon at dawn. Sappy, yes, but true. The playful glances she sent his way hinted at possibilities. The way she'd touched his arm and then left her hand on him had been hot. A caring gesture, but hot nonetheless.

Was this how Adam had felt with Kayla in Fiji?

York hoped not. He wanted to be unattached, free to travel, and available to go out if a woman caught his eye. That wouldn't happen if he had someone waiting at home for him.

Another customer stepped up—a woman wearing scrubs. She must be a nurse.

The store was crowded, but a line hadn't formed yet.

"How may I help you?" York asked.

"One hot chocolate to go," the nurse said.

"I'll make that once I drop these off," Chantelle said as she passed by with two cups of hot chocolate.

He rang up the order. "It'll be just a minute until it's ready."

As he totaled up yet another order for a friendly older customer named Clint, Chantelle delivered the drinks to a couple named Wade and Leah. They were sitting at one of the tables and had introduced themselves when they came in.

York handed over a bag of chocolates. "Here you go. Enjoy."

"Thanks." Clint was one of the owners of a local wine shop. He smiled. "Hope to see you around here more, York. This place could use a little…testosterone."

"Thanks." *I think.*

York was meeting so many people that he'd never remember their names. That was Dakota's gift. One introduction, and she wouldn't forget anyone. She could make a person feel like a long-lost friend five minutes after she met them. That skill she got from their mom.

He and Nevada didn't have the same social abilities. They were too scholarly. At least that was what he liked to think. Their mom claimed they were too much like their dad, which York didn't see at all.

He filled a bag with the colorful chocolate creams that Sage had made for springtime and rang up another order. And another. And another.

Conversations started with each customer who stepped forward. York nodded along, saying an occasional word, but keeping up was proving impossible even though he was aware of whatever Chantelle was doing. She stayed calm and kept a cool head despite the craziness.

When a customer couldn't decide on an anniversary gift for his wife, Chantelle came up with an idea—a bouquet of molded-chocolate flowers, one for each year they'd been married. When another person wanted to take a sick friend a present, she put together a sampler box of different chocolates. A good thing she was there to help. He wouldn't have thought of either of those ideas.

Her excitement when discussing chocolate was palpable, but she didn't show off her knowledge. If she thought he knew the answer, then helping the customer was up to him.

A good thing since that was his responsibility, but he appreciated her being around to answer questions when he couldn't and to tie pretty bows.

Still, he was much too aware of her. If he didn't put some distance between them, he was going to touch her again…or kiss her.

As the clock struck five, the shop's normal closing time when they weren't hosting events, the last customer walked out. He went to the door, clicked the lock in place, and flipped the open sign to closed.

York released a sigh of relief. "Closing time. We did it."

"What are we supposed to do now?" she asked.

He had a few ideas, but none he could say aloud. He looked around at the empty shop. "No clue. I thought Dakota would be back by now because no one taught me how to close, but the info might be in the binder."

"What binder?" Chantelle asked.

He pulled it out from beneath the counter. "This is the employee guide. There must be information on closing. Otherwise, we'll have to wing it and use common sense."

Like turning off the burner for the hot chocolate and washing out the copper pot.

As he flipped the pages, Chantelle peered over his shoulder. She wasn't touching him, but her vanilla scent surrounded him. He had no doubt she would feel good if she pressed her front against his backside.

Focus.

He cleared his throat. "This has what we need."

"What do we do first?" She touched his shoulder with one hand and set off a zing-fest that would have lit up a pinball.

He tried to read the list of items, but the words blurred. Working through a logical process of steps would get him over whatever reaction she'd caused. He blinked and refocused so he could try again.

"Let's start at the top and each do something," she suggested. "We'll be done before we know it."

"Good idea." York should have thought of that except he was still thinking about how nice her touch felt and how delicious she smelled. "I'll take number one."

That dealt with the cash register receipts. He was good at math. Counting would be easy.

"I'll clean the retail area." With the bleach rag and plastic bin for the dishes, she headed toward the tables.

She might have the chocolate touch, but she didn't mind getting her hands dirty or wet. After the tables were finished, she swept and mopped, too.

"What's next?" she asked.

York ran through the list of what he'd done. He'd turned off the burner, cleaned the hot chocolate pot, put away the samples, and washed cups and small plates. "Looks like we're done with the list, but I'm going to text Dakota and ask her."

He went into the back to get his cell phone and typed out a message. **Hope Portia is okay. Shop closed. To-do list from binder done. Anything else we need to do?**

He hit send.

The delivered notice popped up, but no reply.

York returned to the front. He wasn't about to leave the shop until he heard from Dakota, but Chantelle wasn't needed with no customers around. "I'm waiting to hear back from my sister. It's okay for you to take off. There's no need for both of us to stay."

"I don't mind."

He did. "I appreciate that, but didn't you say you wanted to check out Marietta? There's still daylight left."

"I've been on my feet all afternoon." Chantelle removed her apron, went to the closest table, and sat. "The only thing I want to do is sit for a while."

He understood. He'd spent days standing at the base, but

this was different. It wasn't just his feet, though they did hurt. He was tired from smiling and talking and…

His phone beeped. It was from his sister.

Sis1: *Portia is no longer in labor, but she's going to have to stay in the hospital to try to hold off delivery for at least a week, maybe two.*

That was too bad, especially with Rosie Linn, their other coworker, in Los Angeles.

Sis1: *If you followed the list in the binder you can go. I'll stop by on my way home just to double-check everything. Go out the back door to the alley since you don't have keys.*

York: *Sounds good.*

Sis1: *How did things go with Chantelle?*

York: *Fine. She's still here.*

Sis1: *Any chance she can help tomorrow afternoon? I can be there with you in the morning, but I'm supposed to be at the rescue from one to five. Sage is here, and she said she'll pay Chantelle for her time today, as well as any other shifts she covers.*

York reread his sister's last text. Dakota didn't work Friday through Monday, but with Portia in the hospital, schedules would likely change. That didn't mean Chantelle Cummings was the answer to the shop being short-staffed until Rosie Linn returned from Los Angeles.

"Is something wrong?" The concern in Chantelle's voice

carried across the shop.

He took a breath. "Portia needs to stay in the hospital. They're trying to keep her from delivering."

"That's good. Her not delivering early, I mean."

He found himself nodding. Good, but…

His phone beeped.

Sis1: *Did you ask her?*

Her. Chantelle.

Spending more time with the pretty chocolate expert was not the smartest idea. He always did the smart thing—skinny dipping in view of the Officer's Club as a teenager aside—but this…

York was fighting his attraction and losing that battle. Best not to push it by spending more time together, even at work.

"What?" Chantelle asked.

He glanced at his phone again. "Dakota wants to know if you can help out tomorrow from one to five. She can't be here due to something she had planned at the animal rescue where she volunteers. Sage will pay you for any time you work, too."

"Will you be here?"

"Probably," he admitted. "I'm working tomorrow, but I don't know what time."

A beat passed. Then another. "Well, I was going to stop by anyway. Why not?"

He didn't know if the feeling in his gut was anticipation or dread. "I'll text my sister."

York: *Chantelle can work from one to five.*

Sis1: *Tell her thanks.*

York: *Will do.*

Sis1: *Go home and I'll see you there.*

York: *Okay. Call me if you can't find a ride or it gets dark.*

Sis1: *I'm not far away.*

York: *I don't care. You still need to be safe.*

Sis1: *Will do.*

He tucked the phone in his pocket. "Dakota says thanks."

"Happy to help."

Chantelle was going to help him right into making a big mistake. "I...we appreciate that."

"I better get my purse and jacket."

"We have to go out the back," he said. "I don't have a key for the front door."

Two minutes later, the store was dark and they were walking down the alley.

"I'll see you tomorrow." She put on her jacket. "Before you go all he-man, it's still light. The bad guys and zombies aren't out yet. I can walk back to the Graff on my own."

"Okay, but only because the sunlight will keep the vampires away, too."

Smiling, she nodded. "Is a blue shirt and jeans some kind

of uniform employees are supposed to wear?"

"Yes, but don't worry about it."

She perked up. "I have jeans I can wear."

"That'll work." He'd like to see her in jeans, well-worn ones that fit like a glove and showed off her curves. Or not.

"I'll have to check my suitcase for a shirt."

They reached the street and stopped.

"See you tomorrow," she said.

"Looking forward to it."

He shouldn't be, but he was.

The way she smiled up at him with the sun casting a halo around her blond hair was a sight to see, but the feelings she brought out in him were more devilish than angelic.

York watched her cross the street. His stomach twisted. He wished he didn't have to say goodbye right now.

Instead of heading to Dakota's house, he double-backed toward Main Street. He would grab a beer at Grey's Saloon first.

Maybe that would stop him from thinking about his new coworker and how he kept wanting her to bump into him so he could touch her one more time.

SOMETHING WAS RINGING. Chantelle ignored the sound. She wanted to focus on the handsome man with sun-streaked brown hair who was putting a piece of chocolate into her mouth. Except he was blurring.

No. She reached out to stop him from disappearing. *Stay.*

But he was…gone.

Come back. Please.

Eager to return to her dream, she kept her eyes closed and snuggled under the blanket. Maybe sleep would come and the hottie would return. Except maybe this time, he'd bypass giving her chocolate and place his lips on hers.

Please.

The ringing sounded again, an obnoxious, dream-crushing noise that should be outlawed.

She covered her ears. "Go away."

As if whoever was calling could hear her.

Unfortunately, the ringing didn't stop.

With a groan reserved for cancelled flights and lost luggage, she opened her eyes. Blinked. Sighed.

The glow of the digital alarm clock in the dark grabbed her attention.

One o'clock in the morning.

The only person crazy enough to call at this hour would be her cousin Philippe whom she'd emailed earlier. It would be morning in Bayonne.

She reached for her phone on the hotel nightstand. Her hand hit the top, the clock, the lamp base.

No phone.

Chantelle sat, confused, before she remembered. She'd been charging her phone while she ate pizza at the desk.

Getting up didn't appeal to her in the slightest, but she

did anyway. The cool air made her shiver. She found her cell and held it to her ear. "Hello."

"Good morning, cousin." Philippe sounded like he was smiling.

She stretched. "It's still nighttime here."

"But you are a Delacroix. We are night owls."

A Delacroix? She clutched the phone. Her tiredness disappeared faster than her dream had. "Yes, we are."

Saying the words gave her the warm fuzzies. Her cousin considered her part of the family. This called for a celebration. Chocolate. Champagne.

Except…why was he calling her? "Is something wrong?

"No, I read your email and can't believe you've managed to be hired by the chocolate shop there. Well done."

She released the breath she hadn't realized she was holding. "Well, it's more like helping out."

"Yes, that's true, but this will provide you a wonderful experience. Observe everything. Providing excellent customer service is a true skill."

Could this opportunity at Copper Mountain Chocolates be enough to cross off the rest of her uncle's steps? She crossed her fingers. "It's a lovely shop with a very loyal customer base."

"You'll need to determine why they are so loyal."

"That's easy. The chocolate."

"Are you that certain after only a few hours?" Phillip sounded as excited as she felt. Maybe he was looking forward to her coming to France.

"Maybe. Guess I'll find out."

He laughed. "Yes, you will. I spoke with Father, and he's thrilled with what you're doing at the shop."

Yes! She spun around the room. "I told you I'd do everything I could."

"And you are. This will give you an inside view at their unique products, too."

Her cousin was all business. "I'll let you know whether a purchase offer should be drawn up."

"Of course you will."

This was the most relaxed she'd ever hear her cousin sound. She was happy because she had something to do with that happening.

"I'll have a full report for you shortly."

"I can't wait to read it." He sounded genuinely interested in what she had to say, and she tried not to get her hopes up too high. They'd been dashed too many times to do that again. "You're going to fit right in, Chantelle."

Her breath hitched. "That's the nicest thing anyone's said to me."

She had to force the words out due to the thick emotion coating her throat. She didn't care. He was family. Her family.

"Just wait until you're here. Father said you have kept up with your dual citizenship, which will make things much easier."

Thanks, Mom.

The fact her uncle had thought about this told Chantelle it was going to happen. "I don't know why my parents made sure I had that, but I'm glad they did and that my mom made sure I spoke French."

"Me, too."

"Though I'm a little rusty."

Noise sounded in the background. "It's late where you are, and I need to start my day, so I'll let you go. Goodbye, Chantelle."

"Bye, Philippe."

She disconnected from the call and then hugged her phone to her chest. She'd been trying to prove herself to the family, but the lonely days and nights spent working as hard as she could for Uncle Laurent had paid off.

Finally.

Whatever tiredness she'd felt had disappeared, but Chantelle climbed back into bed. She placed her phone on the nightstand next to the clock.

She pulled up the bedcovers and let herself daydream about living in France. There wouldn't be a hottie who looked like York there, but she'd have a family. That was what she'd wanted most of all. Romance and love would follow when she was ready, and then she could live happily ever after.

Chapter Seven

CLEARING A TABLE at the chocolate shop on Friday, York glanced at Dakota, who stood behind the counter. His sister had been watching him all morning. Guess she liked being his boss. Usually, he was the one who took charge of his sisters.

"Am I doing okay?" he asked, trying not to laugh.

She gave him a thumbs-up. "Table looks clean."

"I meant overall."

"Overall, huh?"

The look she gave him was one of pure mischief, much like the constant expression on Zip's face as the cute little cat raced through the house seeking out things he could destroy.

Dakota rubbed her cheek as if trying to figure out something he'd messed up.

He'd opened the door so prepared himself for a full-on frontal assault. "That bad?"

"Not bad."

Okay, maybe he'd misjudged her look. She wasn't a little girl ready to pelt him with snowballs when he wasn't ready.

"But you still can't tie a decent bow to save your life," she said. "You're too generous with the free samples—you aren't supposed to offer seconds. Plus, you use way too much tissue paper in the bags, and you need more practice with the whipped cream."

The girl he remembered who stockpiled snowballs still existed. He grinned. "I'll work on those things."

"Knew my big brother would want to improve." Her expression softened. "You do know how to interact with customers. Even the saltiest of characters walk out of here with smiles, and you clean better than any of us, something I'm sure you learned in the air force because you were never this way at home."

Compliments were always good. "Thanks, sis."

She nodded once in acknowledgement. "Overall, I'd say you're doing pretty good."

"Pretty good?" He would have tossed the bleach rag at her, but he had a feeling Sage wouldn't appreciate that. Instead, he stuck out his chest and did his best superhero impression. "I'm doing incredibly great."

"All hail SuperBro." Dakota laughed. "Though you should know, humility is a virtue."

"Yes, but since I upsold two...did I say two...boxes of truffles and a dozen of those chocolate flowers this morning, modesty is not necessary. Mad skills, oh sister dear. I have them."

She shook her head. "I've created a monster."

"Just wait, it's only my second day." He carried the dirty dishes to the washer in the back. Noticing the kitchen area was empty, he returned to the counter. "Where's Sage?"

She'd been here when he arrived, but must have left when he wasn't paying attention.

"She left," Dakota said. "She's working a split shift today, so she could visit Portia in the hospital and then train Chantelle this afternoon."

"And me."

"Nope. You're off at one today."

Huh? York thought he'd be working with Chantelle again. She'd been on his mind since he'd said goodbye to her yesterday. Not even a beer at Grey's had stopped him from thinking about her. He wanted to spend more time together.

"Why?" he asked. "I thought you needed more help."

"Yes, but we can't wear you out right away. Sage also wants to talk to Chantelle."

"About?"

"Chocolate. What else?"

He could think of a few things he'd rather talk to Chantelle about. None of them had to do with the shop or the chocolate they sold her.

"Sage is thinking of asking Chantelle if she'd be up for another shift or two until Rosie returns."

The thought of working another shift with Chantelle made him smile. "I can finish replacing the windows this afternoon."

Dakota shook her head. "Go do something fun instead. Nevada will be around."

"Around Dustin." The cowboy seemed like a decent guy, but York wasn't used to the changes he'd noticed in Nevada. She was practically giddy all the time when she used to be so quiet with her head stuck in a book. Not a bad thing, just…different. "Those two are inseparable."

"They like being together."

"So do you and Bryce."

"We don't have as much free time as they do, but one of these days…"

Dakota's wistful tone prickled the hair on the back of York's neck. "What?"

She dragged her teeth over her low lip.

Something was up. "Tell me."

"Do you think six months is long enough to know?" she asked.

"Know what?"

"If two people are meant to be together."

York swore under his breath. A weight pressed down on his chest. This was not the kind of question he wanted to answer or advice he should be giving. He looked to the door, but his wish for a customer to enter went unfulfilled.

He shifted his weight between his feet. "Wouldn't Mom be a better person to ask since she's been happily married for over three decades?"

"No way." Dakota's firm tone shut down that idea.

"Mom's already thinking about reception themes…and there hasn't been an official proposal yet."

That sounded like Mom. He stirred the hot chocolate. "I'm really not the person to ask. Remember Jillian?"

"She made the wrong choice. A stupid choice."

He doubted that, but what else could a sister say to her brother?

Dakota placed her hand on his arm. "You've always given me the best advice. I know you will again."

He wiped his clammy hands on the front of the apron. "I'm not very experienced with this, um, relationship stuff. You've had more serious boyfriends than I've had girlfriends."

The one time he'd thought he'd been in love—the forever kind—it hadn't worked out as he'd planned. Jillian hadn't felt the same and had turned down his proposal. Maryland was too far from her family in San Antonio. Now, he wasn't sure what he'd been feeling with her. Love, lust, extreme like?

"Pleeeeease," Dakota said.

His sister had asked, so he would try. "Well, my friend Adam, who went with me to Fiji, knew Kayla was the one for him the day after they met."

"Seriously?"

York nodded. "Adam told me that night she was the woman he'd be marrying, so I should start working on my best-man speech."

Dakota didn't say anything.

York looked at his sister. "Why are you asking?"

"I love Bryce more than I thought possible. I can't imagine him not being a part of my life, but it's a little scary, so I've been wanting us to go slow and take our time. And now Dustin…"

"What about Dustin?"

"He's going to move to New York as soon as the summer season at the Bar V5 ends."

That didn't surprise York as much as he thought it would. The cowboy might be a little rough around the edges, but Dustin seemed to understand Nevada in a way few did. The fact he drove from the ranch to their house when he couldn't get hold of her due to a misplaced or dead cell phone told York how much the man cared for his youngest sister.

"Makes sense," York said. "Dustin can teach riding lessons and take college courses anywhere."

"He's a cowboy used to riding the range. He's going to hate the Big Apple."

"Probably. But that's up to him to figure out. He'll only be there until Nevada gets her PhD."

Dakota nodded, but she seemed to want to say more.

York tried to figure out what Dakota was thinking, but she kept her feelings well hidden. Always had. "Are you worried about Nevada?"

"Not worried, but they only got together in February

and are already making plans for the future. Big ones. It makes me wonder if it's time for Bryce and me…"

York had no idea what he needed to say, but he couldn't brush this off. "There isn't a set time table for relationships, sis. Everyone is different. Knowing right away like Adam doesn't make his feelings better or stronger. Just like waiting doesn't mean yours are weaker. It sounds sappy, but all you can do is follow your heart. Remember how Great-Aunt Alice used to say that."

Dakota nodded. "She was smart like you and Nevada."

"You're smart, too. It runs in the family." He set down the spoon. "I'm sorry I'm not more helpful."

She hugged him. "You're the perfect help. As always."

"Keep me posted on what you decide. In case I need to work on a brother-of-the-bride speech."

She swatted his arm. "There's no such thing."

York winked. "There should be."

"You just want the spotlight."

"I want you to be happy."

"I am. More than I've ever been."

"Then maybe that's your answer." York couldn't believe he was saying those words to Dakota, but she'd never seemed as happy and loved as she was with Bryce.

Another nod. "Adam found his one true love in Fiji. What about you?"

She sounded more like their mom. "I had fun. That was the plan. Come June, I'm ready for a substantial change.

THE CHOCOLATE TOUCH

Traveling, working at different sites, having more fun."

"The air force didn't turn out like you expected."

"No, but it was good."

The years he'd spent in the service had been good for him, but he'd never gotten to prove himself the way he'd wanted, to show his dad that joining the air force had been where he'd make his mark.

"I just got tired of following orders, doing what someone else wanted me to do, thinking I'd be on the brink of doing more or going somewhere else, and then staying where I was. Things got better when I was the one giving orders, but I still felt stuck." He half-laughed. "It would have been perfect for Dad or a family guy, but I was too restless."

"You still are."

"Which is why I accepted the consulting job and not a corporate one."

The bell on the door jingled.

"Welcome to Copper Mountain Chocolates," Dakota said.

Chantelle entered the shop. "Hi."

Her blond hair was pulled back into a single braid. She wore a dark blue short-sleeved shirt and a pair of jeans that hugged the curve of her hips.

He'd never seen her dressed so casually, but he liked it. A lot. "Hey."

"How is Portia?" Chantelle asked.

"Keeping that baby from celebrating an early birthday,"

121

Dakota said. "I'm sure Sage will update us when she gets here. You'll be working with her today."

"Great." Chantelle sounded pleased. "We can talk chocolate."

Dakota nodded. "That's what Sage said."

Chantelle moved closer to the counter. "What about you, York?"

"I get the afternoon off." He tried to sound happy about that, but wasn't sure if he succeeded or not. He wanted to work with Chantelle.

Something—disappointment, perhaps?—flashed across her face. "Oh. I, um, thought—"

"Me, too." Maybe talking chocolate wasn't the only thing on her mind. Maybe he was. That made him smile. "Another time."

She nodded. "I'll put my stuff in the back and put on an apron."

As she walked past, he enjoyed the view of her butt. Yeah, jeans looked as good on her as the skirts she wore.

"Something I should know?" Dakota asked in her which-one-of-you-is-the-guilty-dog-or-cat voice.

York wasn't about to fall for that. "About?"

She motioned to the back. "Her."

"No. But what can I say? I'm a guy. I look at women."

"That wasn't a look, that was a leer." Dakota didn't believe him. "You sure nothing's going on?"

"Nothing is going on." Unfortunately.

But seeing Chantelle again made him wonder if there would be anything wrong about two coworkers having a drink together. To talk shop, er, chocolate, and whatever else happened to come up.

That wouldn't be a date.

More of an off-site meeting.

She'd bumped into him at the bookstore. Maybe he could do the same when she got off work.

FIVE O'CLOCK ARRIVED quickly. Spending time with Sage today made Chantelle feel as if she were attending the chocolate academy again. She'd loved every minute of it. Now she went through the steps to close the store under Sage's watchful gaze.

Copper Mountain Chocolates' owner was meticulous and a perfectionist. No wonder their chocolate was so delicious. Sage had lofty standards for her products and the staff who sold it. She'd poured her heart into the business and nurtured the relationships with her customers. She didn't seem unhappy or ready to do something different, but Chantelle wanted to confirm that.

As for Sage's processes and recipes, those weren't topics open for discussion. Any questions had been shut down immediately. No insider scoop. Chantelle would put that in her report. She hoped Philippe and Uncle Laurent weren't disappointed, but the customer-service experience, as her cousin had mentioned, had been priceless, and she'd be getting more. Sage had asked her to take shifts until Rosie returned from her trip.

Chantelle had enough information to write her report, and she would, but she was also happy to help and learn more. And maybe, just maybe, she'd get to work another shift with York.

Thinking his name put a bounce to her step. Silly, yes, but she had a harmless crush on the guy. He was fun to be around and good looking. Who wouldn't like him?

"You better watch where you're going or you might bump into somebody."

The sound of York's voice made her stop. He stood in the middle of the sidewalk directly in her path. If he hadn't said anything, she might have walked right into him. Again. "I was just—"

"What?"

Saying she was thinking about him would make her sound interested. She was, but Chantelle didn't want him to know that. "Lost in my thoughts."

That was the truth. He didn't need to know her thoughts were about him.

"What are you doing?" she asked.

"I installed another window for Dakota and then decided to take a walk downtown." He rocked back on his heels. "It's Happy Hour at Grey's Saloon. Want to get a drink?"

"Sure." The word popped out before she had time to

think about the reasons she shouldn't do this. No problem. One drink wouldn't hurt anything. It wasn't like he'd asked her out to dinner.

"Grey's is down one block." He fell in step with her. The same as he had the other night. "Is this your first view of downtown Marietta in the daylight?"

"Other than walking to the chocolate shop. I like what I see."

For a little after five on a Friday night, the sidewalks were more crowded than she would have expected. People went in and out of shops and cafes.

"Quaint," she decided.

"You should see this place at Christmastime. I was here in December a couple of years ago. The town knows how to do up the holidays."

"Must be nice. I'm not a big Christmas fan."

"Why not?"

Not trusting her voice, she shrugged.

"Hard with your mom gone?" he asked.

Chantelle nodded. "My dad's dead, too."

"Oh, man." York put his arm around her shoulder and pulled her close. "Any other family around?"

"In France. I didn't know them until a few years ago. We're slowly reconnecting."

He dropped his arm but stayed close by her side. "That's a long way from Boston, but it's great you have them. Family is important. We are spread out and don't always spend the holidays together, but last Christmas, we opened gifts while all on Skype. It was more fun than I thought it would be."

"I'll remember that." At least Chantelle hoped she would. She was still thinking about his arm around her.

A couple ahead of them held hands. The blond woman had a leash strap around her wrist of a Yorkshire Terrier dressed in a hot pink sweater and bows on its ears. The little dog glanced back and barked. A sharp, squeaky kind of sound.

"Clementine," the woman said with a firm but loving tone. "No barking."

The dog didn't seem to care. She looked forward and pranced away as if she were the queen of Marietta. She could be. The bling on her collar and leash could fill a crown.

"I think that's one of the dogs adopted through the rescue where Dakota works," York said. "The name sounds like one she mentioned to me."

"You and your sisters are close."

He nodded. "We tease each other unmercifully, but yeah, I'd call us close. We don't spend a lot of time together, but the three of us were army brats and we moved a lot. Sometimes we only had each other until we made new friends."

"You're lucky to have each other."

"Very," he said. "Your family in France. Is there anyone your age?"

"A cousin. His name is Philippe, and we text almost every day. He's different from me. All business. A workaholic."

"Tell him to stop and taste the chocolate."

She laughed. York had no idea how apt that phrase was in this situation. "I have, but he thinks he knows better."

"Guys always do."

"You?"

"Sometimes. Well, most of the time. But I get why your cousin is like that." He looked around. "The one thing I've noticed about Marietta is how the pace is slower here. No one's in a rush like on the East Coast. People not only stop to smell the roses, but they also pick the flowers to give to others."

"That's nice. Maybe we should slow down."

A grin spread across his face. "Too late. We're almost there. But when I leave Marietta, I'm going to remember not to be in such a hurry all the time."

"Where will you live?"

"All over. I'll be a computer consultant and travel to clients. Dakota is storing my stuff until I figure out another place to live."

"Just you and a suitcase."

The smile on his face told he was happy about this. "I've been wanting to travel like this for a while. I can't wait."

They were so different, and any desire to see if something could develop from her crush disappeared. York Parker wasn't looking for anything beyond right now when all she could think about was the future.

"I was like you three years ago," she admitted. "I had fun at first, but now I'm tired of traveling and staying in hotels. I'm ready to settle down and create a home."

"In Boston."

"France. My mother was French. Some petition or something gave me dual citizenship."

"Ah, so that's where the name Chantelle comes from."

She nodded. "My father was American."

"Excuse me." A man in a cowboy hat pushed a stroller toward them. Every passerby greeted the smiling man by name, which was Nate.

She stepped away from York to let the man and child pass between them, but continued walking. Seeing the grinning, drooling toddler in the stroller made her think of Portia.

Chantelle glanced back at the father and child. "I hope Portia is going to be okay. Not just with the early labor, but long term."

York moved closer to Chantelle again. "Nevada said Portia's thinking about giving the baby up for adoption."

"I don't think I could do that myself, but everybody's situation is different. Being a single parent is hard." Chantelle thought about her dad. "I was twelve when my mom died, and my dad had a tough time with her death. They were so in love, and she did everything for him. I tried to help with the laundry, house, cooking, and the garden, but she was just so good at everything and I was—"

"A kid."

An unexpected smile tugged at her lips. "When you put it that way, I guess I did okay."

"I'm sure you did." He opened the door for her. Country music played. "Welcome to Grey's Saloon."

She entered to the smell of beer, the sound of conversations, and the sight of cowboys—men in worn jeans and scuffed boots, with cowboy hats sitting nearby.

York motioned to an empty booth.

As she slid across the bench seat, he remained standing. "What would you like?"

She usually enjoyed a glass of wine, but this seemed more like a beer, whiskey, or shot kind of place. "A beer. Lager or IPA, if they have either."

"I'd have taken you more for a Chardonnay drinker."

"Pinot Gris, but when in Marietta…"

He smiled. "Be right back."

The place was like something out of a movie, complete with a pool table and more good-looking men than she'd seen in one place in a long time. But none of them were as handsome as York.

He placed two pints of beer on the table, and that was when she realized he'd paid. She would have to get the next round. Well, if there was one.

"They had a lager," he said. "I decided to try it, too."

"Thanks." She took a sip. "Good."

He drank. "It is."

Someone cheered. Must be the people at the pool table.

"Come here often?" she asked.

"I'm never in town long enough to come here that much. There's also Flint Works, which is a brewery at the Depot or the bar at the Graff, but I like Grey's the best. It's comfortable and safe, if no cowboys are fighting, and reasonably priced."

"Let's hope the cowboys remain under control."

"I've never seen a fight myself, but Dustin—he's my sister Nevada's boyfriend—warned me."

"Is he the one who won the vacation and gave it to you?"

"Yeah, he and Nevada had done much of the quest together, but it turned out Nevada was ineligible to win since Dakota worked at Copper Mountain Chocolates, which was a sponsor. That didn't matter in the end. Dustin said meeting my sister was the best prize."

"That's sweet."

"Especially since he seems to mean it."

"Protective big brother."

"Always." York wiped a bead of condensation from his glass. "I brought Dustin a few gifts from Fiji to say thanks, but I wish I could find out who donated the trip."

"That's some donation."

"An anonymous one. The first thing I did when I arrived at Dakota's house was send a thank-you to the law firm that represents the donor. I was hoping I might get a name, but I never received a reply from the office."

"You haven't been here that long."

"True."

"This is important to you."

He nodded. "I'd like to say thank you."

"They might have a reason for wanting to remain anonymous."

"That's what Dakota said. Someone made a big donation to the animal rescue where she volunteers, and she thinks it's the same person." York pulled out his cell phone and showed her a list of names. "This is who I think could be the unsub."

"Unsub."

"Unknown subject aka the anonymous donor."

He was hot and geeky. An appealing combination. "You do watch a lot of crime shows."

"Now it's time to solve my own mystery."

She read over the list:

Josiah Whittaker
Troy Sheehan
Jasper Flint
Nate Vaughn
Walt Grayson

"Wait a minute." She put York's phone on the table. "You have Walt Grayson listed?"

He shrugged. "Dakota and Bryce swear it isn't him."

"You asked them?"

"Yes. They said Walt has money from selling his house

and business back in Pennsylvania, but not that much to give away. Dakota also thinks Walt is so good-natured and social that he would have let it slip if he were doing that. He's not good at keeping secrets."

Chantelle stared over the lip of her glass. "Yet, you're keeping him on this list."

"They're just names. I don't have much evidence to go on."

"But you're looking for clues."

"Yes, but it's an effort in futility." He drank. "There's not much else I can do until I hear back from the law office."

"Give it a week or two."

"You're more patient than I am."

She thought about the past three years. All the effort she'd put in. "Sometimes you have to be to get what you want."

"I'll have to try it." He raised his glass. "To patience."

Staring into her eyes, he tapped his glass against hers and then drank. He licked his lips, and she wanted a taste of him.

"Hungry?" he asked.

His question caught her off guard. "For food?"

"Yes, but if you have something else in mind?"

His tone was sexy and playful. Heat scorched her cheeks.

She drank. That didn't cool her down. "Food would be good."

"The food is good here, but want to go somewhere else that isn't so noisy?

"Um, sure." Drinks, now dinner. This was feeling more like a date. Would kissing be next?

Chantelle wasn't sure she wanted to know the answer.

AN HOUR LATER, York's stomach was full after a delicious Italian dinner at Rocco's on First Street, but the best part was sitting at the table with Chantelle. He hadn't had such a nice evening with a woman in months. Maybe years.

He walked toward the door with Chantelle at his side. "I'm glad we're walking."

She nodded. "I don't think I'll need to eat breakfast."

He opened the door, and she stepped outside.

The temperature was in the mid-fifties. Comfortable with no breeze. He would have expected Montana to be colder in early May, but he'd never been here this time of year. If it were cooler, he'd have a reason to put his arm around Chantelle to keep her warm.

Not a date.

Except tonight felt like one.

"This has been fun," he said.

"I've had a wonderful time." She walked at a leisurely pace. She didn't seem to be in any kind of rush to get back to the hotel. That was fine by him.

"Thanks for dinner." The street lamps cast shadows on her face, but he could still see her flushed cheeks. "The food was incredible."

"And you got your wine."

"I did, but the beer at Grey's wasn't bad."

"The wine was better."

"I agree." She looked around. "I can't wait to explore Marietta tomorrow."

"Aren't you working?"

"From ten to one. I'll have time after that."

As they walked, the space between them narrowed. He liked being near her. "If you want company, let me know. I haven't had a chance to play tourist yet."

"I will."

He hoped she would.

York stopped at the intersection of First and Front. The Graff Hotel was across the street, but he didn't want to say goodnight. Not yet.

"Want to keep walking?" he asked.

She nodded. "It's a beautiful night."

The distance between them closed even more until his arm bumped hers. Finally. He laced his fingers with hers. "This okay?"

Another nod.

Good. York been dying to touch her for hours. He wasn't disappointed. Her hand with its soft skin fit nicely in his.

They passed the pizza parlor on the corner. The place looked packed inside. Customers carried out pizza boxes. Others waited by the door to get a table.

"I had dinner there a couple of nights ago," he said.

"I took a couple of slices home for dinner last night." She squeezed his hand. "But I think you've spoiled me after tonight."

He wanted to spoil her more.

Wheels against asphalt sounded. Two boarders were speeding toward them.

York pulled Chantelle out of the way and against a building.

As the boarders raced by, neither glanced their way or muttered an apology.

"Punks," he called after them.

The boys didn't look back.

His arm was still around Chantelle. "You okay?"

"Fine."

He was, too, because he was standing so close to her. She fit nicely against him. Her head came to his chin. Her vanilla scent made him feel like he'd drank more than he had.

She licked her lips, just a quick swipe of her tongue, nothing really, but a burst of need rushed through him. He lowered his arms so he wasn't touching her. It didn't help.

He still wanted to kiss her. "Chantelle—"

Her mouth was on his before he could say another word.

Chantelle's surprising, eager kiss was exactly what he needed. Moving his lips against hers, he wrapped his arms around her to bring her closer. This was no tentative get-to-know-you kiss. They'd passed that stage two seconds in. Maybe one. She hadn't hesitated, and he liked her initiative.

He really liked how she kissed.

Her hands were in his hair. She kept devouring his lips. Or maybe it was the other way. He couldn't be sure, but he didn't care.

Nothing mattered right now except this moment. This kiss. This woman.

He'd never tasted anything better. Sweet with a hint of cabernet, the wine they'd shared over dinner.

The fact she'd kissed him first and kept on kissing him with no sign of slowing down was a total turn-on.

Forget having the chocolate touch.

Chantelle's lips were going to drive him crazy.

Her chest pressed up to his, and the rapid beat of her heart thumped against his. The need for a kiss he'd felt moments ago erupted into a blazing heat…for more.

Slow down.

Good advice, but instead, York deepened the kiss, exploring her mouth with his tongue. She wiggled her hips against him.

His control slipped.

An ache inside increased.

Be careful.

He hadn't lost his entire brain function, but if she kept moving her hips like that, all bets were off. Except he wasn't ready to go all in. Not tonight.

York loosened his arms and took half a step back. That put space between their bodies, but not enough. He kissed her one last time before stepping back more.

Gorgeous and sexy.

Those two words described Chantelle. Her eyes were wide and full of the same desire running through him. Her swollen lips were puckered, as if to say she wanted more kisses. Her breathing was uneven and heavy like his.

A slow, sassy grin curved her lips. "Dessert with no calories. I could go for seconds."

Being in control had to be overrated. He kissed her again.

Chapter Eight

KISSING YORK WAS even better the second time. She hadn't ever felt this crazy need to have her lips against another person's—as if his kisses were as vital to her as oxygen or chocolate—but she did with him.

They just seemed to…fit.

Perfectly.

His lips moved over hers, tasting and teasing. She couldn't get enough of his kisses or of him.

Oh, she knew kissing probably wasn't the best idea, but she didn't want to stop, even if common sense and logic told her the only things she'd leave Marietta with were a few good memories and possibly a broken heart.

She would focus on the memories.

Particularly the ones from this kiss.

A moan escaped her lips. York deepened the kiss. He made her feel special, as if only her kiss would do.

With her hands on his shoulders, she clung to him, not caring if that made her look needy or desperate.

She was.

For more kisses.

And for him.

Thank goodness his mouth continued to press against hers. That was all she wanted.

Little squeaks and noises sounded.

From her?

Most likely.

How long had it been since a man had kissed her so thoroughly?

Um, never.

She ran her tongue around York's mouth. He tasted warm and salty and like something pure male. This—he—was her new favorite dessert.

She wanted to be closer, but something held her back. His effect on her had been so unexpected she'd gotten carried away with that first kiss, awash in feelings and responses.

The same things could easily happen this time, except she was trying to be more careful. Keeping her guard up. Well, halfway up.

She feared her efforts were failing because every touch of his lips and his hands made her feel so good, as if she'd found a piece of herself that had been missing for far too long.

She lowered a hand to his back. Her fingers ran over the muscles beneath. So strong. Giving into the feelings would be so easy, but she couldn't. She had to keep herself from letting go completely, if only a sliver of control remained.

She wanted his kisses, but anything more would be stupid.

Stupid.

The word resonated through her.

Don't be stupid.

She pulled away. Reluctantly.

His hands fell to his sides, and a part of her wished he was touching her. Still, the hunger in his eyes sent a rush of power and pride through her. She'd put that look there, but she needed to be smart about this. About him. "Thanks."

"My pleasure."

Hers, too.

The street came alive with the sounds of cars driving by and a horn honking off in the distance. The scent of pizza from the restaurant next door scented the air. Now that he wasn't touching her, the air felt cooler against her heated skin.

And York.

His hair was a mess, and he'd never looked sexier. Was this what he looked like when he woke up in the morning?

She'd never know that, but she reached up and combed her fingers through his hair. Damage control, she told herself, not to feel the soft strands again.

"There." She finished combing his hair. "Now you don't look so—"

"Thoroughly kissed like you do?" His grin spread quickly

and crinkled the corner of his eyes.

Swoon worthy was the only to describe his smile. She cleared her dry throat. "Yes."

"I'd offer to fix your hair, but I'd only make it worse."

Lips tingling, Chantelle had no doubt she must look as thoroughly kissed as he did. She felt that way, a bit dazed and lightheaded, too.

"I'll settle for this." He took her hand in his and kissed the top.

The romantic gesture brought a sigh to her lips.

He kept her hand near his mouth. "You like?"

"Very much." Her gaze slanted to the store window so she could see how messed up her hair was.

A lovely white lace dress caught her attention. Next to that one was a pink confection of delicate applique flowers and crystals. So perfect. Her breath caught.

Wedding dresses. They hadn't kissed in front of any store, but a bridal salon called Married in Marietta.

A sign? She gulped. A reminder of what she truly wanted?

As York kissed each of her knuckles, images formed in her mind. The small chapel at her uncle's chateau. Flowers everywhere. A harp playing.

The fantasy sharpened. The scent of flowers. Twinkling white lights. Flickering candles. Romantic music. The clinking of silverware against crystal.

A wedding.

Her wedding.

No. No. No.

A crush was one thing. Picturing a wedding after one—make that two—hot kisses was bad. The worst kind of bad. Psycho-chick bad.

Chill.

"What do you want to do now?" he asked, still holding onto her hand.

"I..." Her gaze bounced between the two dresses that represented her dream of finding forever love and a happily ever after versus having fun with York for a brief amount of time. His kisses made her feel a way she hadn't before. He was handsome and charming, and she'd enjoyed herself tonight.

But...

The thoughts running through her head could fill a 128-gigabyte flash drive.

Chantelle knew what she wanted. Not tonight with York, but for her future. She'd known for the past three years. She didn't want to make a mistake when she was so close to making her dream come true.

"Tonight's been great," she said sincerely. "But I have work to do."

"That's true dedication on a Friday night." He sounded disappointed, but he held onto her hand. "Let's get you back to the hotel."

"Thanks." Chantelle felt bad because he'd done nothing

wrong. She was the one who'd freaked out and gone bridal on him. "I worked this afternoon, so I have a few things to do tonight."

"I understand."

Did he? She hoped so.

"Do you still want company while you play tourist tomorrow?" he asked.

"Yes." The word flew from her lips like the free chocolate passed out at her book signing. *Uh-oh.* No would have been the smarter answer, but the smile he rewarded her with was worth saying yes.

"Meet you in the hotel lobby at one-thirty?" he asked.

"Sounds good."

Playing tourist would be fun. They could check out the town and local attractions. No need to kiss again. Or hold hands.

Though she liked the feel of his warm hand around hers and was glad he hadn't let go.

Stop.

A romance, even a casual one, was not what she wanted or needed right now. She needed to work on the report for her uncle and remain focused on getting to Bayonne. Distractions—even short-term ones—wouldn't be good.

York stopped outside the main doors of the hotel. "If I kiss you again, I'm not going to want to stop, so I'll say goodnight here."

She appreciated his honesty. He was a sweet guy. A

sweet, hot guy.

"Thanks again for tonight."

Unsure what to say, she hesitated. The biggest problem was she didn't want tonight to end. Part of her wanted him to stay with her longer, but that couldn't happen. Not just tonight.

Time to draw the line.

"I'm looking forward to tomorrow," she continued. "Though maybe we shouldn't, um, kiss again. It was great. Amazing. But I'm not looking for, um, anything like that."

He released her hand as if he were holding onto a lit match about to burn his fingers. "Yeah, me, either."

"Good," she said a little quickly.

"Yes, good."

Okay, they agreed. Why was there still an icky feeling in her chest?

"No worries. You can never have too many friends," he added. "Goodnight, Chantelle."

Being friends would be okay, wouldn't it? "Goodnight, York."

As she walked toward the hotel's entrance, she repeated the word *friend* in her mind. About to step into the hotel, she glanced back.

York was standing in the same place and watching her.

Chantelle gave him a half-hearted wave. Her stomach hadn't settled and her lips still tingled, but no big deal. All she had to do was put his hot kisses behind her and think of him as her friend.

How hard could that be?

WHAT WAS WRONG with him? As York walked to his sister's house, he kicked a small rock on the sidewalk. The stone flew onto a yard twenty feet away and thudded against the grass.

You can never have too many friends.

That was the stupidest thing he could have said. Kissing Chantelle had been incredible, and then he'd gone and parked himself in the friend zone.

Ugh.

His lips wanted to stage a protest at the thought of not kissing Chantelle again.

Friends…

What had he been thinking?

York couldn't blame alcohol. A beer at Grey's and then wine at dinner wouldn't cause him to say that. But he knew the reason. He'd wanted to remove the wariness from her eyes and put the smile back on her face. She'd seemed…freaked out.

Maybe we shouldn't, um, kiss again. It was great. Amazing. But I'm not looking for, um, anything like that.

Face it, he wasn't looking for "anything like that" either. Although her definition could be different from his. The chemistry between them wasn't just strong—it was over-whelming.

Combustible.

Something unexpected, but not entirely unwelcome, if he were being honest. He understood why the kisses had shaken up Chantelle. He'd felt nothing like that with the women in Fiji or any of the women he'd dated in the past. And a relationship—unless super casual—was the last thing he wanted. Chantelle didn't seem like the casual type.

He half-laughed.

Come June, he would finally be living the life he'd dreamed about. Being friends might not be what he initially wanted, but maybe this had worked out for the best.

The last thing he wanted was for Chantelle to feel uncomfortable around him. He never wanted to be *that* guy.

He knew how to be a good friend. Having two younger sisters had taught him lots. He'd just never started off kissing a female friend or wanting to kiss her again.

First time for everything.

York dragged his hand through his hair.

He knew what he'd do to start their friendship off on the right foot. He would arrange something fun for them to do besides checking out the town. Something to show Chantelle that all was good. And he knew who could help him.

Dustin Decker. He worked at a dude ranch that catered to vacationers. If anyone knew about tourist activities, Nevada's boyfriend would.

York picked up his pace. When he reached Dakota's front door, he was surprised to see so many lights on in the house. He expected his sisters to be out with their boyfriends. He walked inside.

"Hey." Bryce waved from the couch. He held onto a bowl of popcorn. Fang, a chestnut-brown dog with a graying muzzle, lay at his feet and Zip, the newest arrival, sat on his shoulder. "Dakota and I are going to watch a movie if you want to join us."

"Thanks, but finishing up those windows this afternoon wore me out. I'm going to call it an early night."

"There's pizza in the kitchen."

"Thanks, but I ate already."

Dakota entered the living room with two glasses in her hand. "Where did you eat?"

"Rocco's."

"Delicious food. Were you out with Nevada and Dustin?"

York didn't want to answer that. He hadn't even thought about the consequences to his sister and the chocolate shop before or after he'd kissed Chantelle. A good thing they were only going to be friends. He gave a slight shake of his head and hoped that would be the end of Dakota's questions. "Enjoy your movie. I'm going upstairs."

"There's a letter for you on the hall table." Dakota sat next to Bryce. "It's from the law office in Bozeman that the mysterious benefactor uses. Did you contact them?"

Chantelle had been correct when she told him to be patient. He picked up the letter and opened the flap. "I sent a thank-you note to give to whoever donated the vacation package. I wanted to acknowledge the person's generosity."

"The rescue did the same," Dakota said. "The staff and volunteers all signed a card. We included pictures of the animals with their new families and a receipt with our tax id information on it, but almost six months later, we're no closer to finding out who that person is."

He waved the envelope. "Maybe the answer is in here."

York pulled out a piece of ivory-colored paper. The law firm must have a big stationery budget to afford such thick, heavy paper. He read the letter. *Dear Mr. Parker. Thank you,* yadda, yadda, yadda. *We are sending your note,* yadda, yadda, yadda, *and appreciate your gratitude, but please understand that our client prefers to remain anonymous.*

York sighed. "I can't believe this."

Dakota had gotten up from the couch and joined him in the hallway. "Is there a name?"

"No. Nothing but a letter saying my note was passed on to the benefactor."

She touched his arm. "You're disappointed."

"A little," he admitted. "I want the donor to know how much I appreciate what he, she, or they did. I'm assuming the person wants to remain anonymous for a reason, but it would be great to thank them in person."

"That's how everyone at Whiskers and Paw Pals feels. The Thanksgiving donation has made such a difference for the animals and the facility. Sending a thank-you card doesn't feel like enough."

"That's how I feel, too."

She lowered her arm. "I think whoever donated your vacation is the same person who donated to the rescue in November. I have no proof, but I can't see two different individuals picking the same law firm in another town when there are perfectly good attorneys in Marietta."

"I've asked before, but any clue who it might be?"

"None. It could be any one of the wealthy folk living around Marietta or one of the many who vacation here."

"I guess the donor's identity is meant to be a mystery." York fanned the letter. "I tried."

"You did, and you thanked that person. Can't do much more with nothing else to go on. Lori, the director at the shelter, told us that we needed to respect our donor's wish for privacy."

York understood that. "This is over as far as I'm concerned. Go back to your movie and your boyfriend."

Dakota beamed. "You don't have to tell me twice."

As she headed to the couch, York went upstairs to the guest bedroom. He tossed the letter onto the queen-sized bed, sat, and removed his shoes.

Wait a minute. He stared at the letter. That wasn't one piece of paper, but two.

No wonder the paper felt so thick. A second page was attached to the back of first one. He pulled them apart.

The second letter was addressed to Judge A. Kingsley,

who lived on Bramble Lane in Marietta. York read.

Dear Judge Kingsley:

Enclosed is a note from York Parker, who was the recipient of the luxurious vacation package to Fiji you donated to The Valentine Quest. Per your request, we did not share your identity, but I assured Mr. Parker that his correspondence would be passed on.

Please do not hesitate to call if you have any needs in the future.

Sincerely,
Stanley Price

That was the same name of the lawyer who'd signed York's letter, but the copier had foiled Stanley Price's attempt to keep the benefactor's identity a secret.

Judge A. Kingsley.

York had never heard the name before, but he would learn more about the man and do so carefully. Too much was at stake to do this otherwise.

He folded the two pages and put them into his computer bag—a safe place.

If someone at the law office besides Stanley Price had let this mistake happen, that person could be fired for a printer error. York didn't want that to happen. Nor did he want the judge to stop making donations—ones that helped individuals like him and the community at large—if his identity became public.

That meant York couldn't tell anybody.

Including Dakota.

Keeping secrets had been part of his former job. He would find the answers he wanted, and somehow figure out a way to show his appreciation for the vacation package he'd received.

Maybe Dustin could not only help with making plans for tomorrow, but also share some information about the judge.

York pulled out his phone and typed a text to Nevada aka Sis2: **Tell Dustin to call me. Have questions for him.**

SATURDAY, AFTER TOURING Marietta with York, Chantelle sat in the passenger seat of his crossover SUV. The interior felt…confining. That was the reason she was uncomfortable. It had nothing to do with how good York looked in faded jeans and a plain T-shirt. Or the way his soap or aftershave— a clean, fresh scent with a hint of mint—teased and reminded her of their kiss last night.

She'd been able to keep her distance from York and add more space between them if she'd drifted too close to him as they visited various places in town, window shopped, explored the park, and strolled down Bramble Lane, which was lined with big, old houses.

Not now. Maybe she should roll down the window.

"How long a drive is it?" She had no idea where they were going, but she hoped it wasn't too far.

He flicked on his blinker and turned the car away from the town. "It's about a forty-minute drive."

That was longer than she thought. He'd told her about making plans for the late afternoon. She had no idea what he had in mind, only that he'd promised it would be fun.

She was all for fun.

Fun with her friend.

But a friend didn't keep wanting to smell another friend. She was trying to keep things friendly, but that was becoming harder to do being so close to him, and noticing the way the fabric of his short sleeves stretched over his muscles, or how his profile showed off his long eyelashes or...

This was going to drive her crazy.

Think of something to say... anything.

"Where are we going again?" she asked.

"I haven't told you."

"I was hoping you'd just forgotten to tell me."

York glanced her way, but then returned his gaze to the road. "Don't you like surprises?"

"Not many people in my life to surprise me these days." She cringed at how that must sound. "But that's my fault. I'm either working or traveling or both."

"That sounds like what my life will be like soon."

"You're welcome to it. I can't wait to stay in one place."

Soon.

She stared out the window. "Not much out this way."

"Ranches and livestock, but Paradise Valley has some of

the most beautiful scenery you'll see around here."

"And stars."

That brought a smile to his face. Not that one had been lacking today, but none had reached his eyes like this one. "When the sky is dark enough, you'll see them."

"Tonight?"

"Depends on how late things go." He gave her a sideward glance. "That okay?"

"Sure." It was a little late to say no, but that didn't stop her anxiety from rising. She clasped her hands on her lap.

"It's nice seeing what's outside of town," she said. "Today, when customers found out I'm not from Marietta, or that this is my first trip to Montana, they told me what to see. A few gave me history lessons. People love this place."

"Dakota does. She's lived here six, almost seven years."

"Some have been here their entire lives. I heard lots of stories. That made the time go fast." She realized how that must have sounded. "I had fun during my shift, but I'm not used to working retail. Not easy work."

"It's been an adjustment for me, too. At least you're getting paid."

"I, uh, declined Sage's offer to pay me."

"Why?

Chantelle didn't know where to start. "Portia ending up in the hospital wasn't planned."

"No, we thought she had two, maybe three, more weeks until the baby arrived, but that's nice of you to help."

It wasn't the only reason. "I also didn't want there to be any conflict of interest. I want to write a review about Copper Mountain Chocolates so being paid wouldn't be right."

"That's smart."

"I try to be." She'd also mentioned to Sage about consulting and doing a business analysis, but no questions had been asked, so Chantelle hadn't offered any details.

"In exchange for my volunteering," Chantelle added. "Sage said I can write about the experience at the shop and take photographs, too."

"Nice."

"I'm for sure doing a review, but I might be able to write an article for a magazine or my blog."

"You'll know all the products by the time you leave."

Chantelle already did. She thought about telling him about her family—well, soon-to-be family—but he wasn't that into chocolate and she'd just met him. Kissing last night, aside. He wasn't a chocolate connoisseur, so what would he care?

"I'm sure I'll have tasted everything before I have to leave."

He turned off the main road and drove under a wooden sign that read Bar V5 Dude Ranch.

"Dude ranch?" she asked.

"We'll be there shortly. This is a long driveway."

The minutes passed. "What are we doing at a dude

ranch?"

"Being dudes?"

"I look like a dude?"

"No." The word came out sharp and swift. "Nevada's boyfriend Dustin Decker is a wrangler here. Eli, the man from the shop the day Portia went to the hospital, is too."

Chantelle remembered Eli. "So many cowboys in Marietta, real ones—not wannabes."

"Not only in Marietta. Montana is full of them. Dustin is a former rodeo champion."

"I've never been to a rodeo." She'd been born and raised in Pennsylvania. Growing up, vacations had never been extravagant trips and never west of the Mississippi River. Writing about chocolate had given her the opportunity to explore more states and other countries, but every trip revolved around work and a lot of time was spent in her hotel room.

York followed a curved section of the driveway that split off to the left and wrapped in front of the three-story luxurious lodge-like structure. A front porch ran the width of the building. Flower baskets hung along the porch railing, and comfortable rockers and a swing waited for occupants.

"Ranch?" She stared out the windshield. "This looks more like a lavish mountain hotel."

York parked between a sedan and a minivan. There were also pickup trucks. Families and couples walked around.

"I've never stayed here. Too expensive for me, but I

toured the horse barn a couple of Christmases ago with my sisters. Each year, they hang custom wreaths on each horse stall. Lots of photo opportunities, gingerbread cookies, and hot cocoa or cider. The ranch does activities up right."

He sounded like a tourist brochure. It was cute. Was he a little nervous? Chantelle liked the idea that she wasn't the only one on edge.

"I'm looking forward to whatever this is." Chantelle was. She reminded herself this wasn't a date, just two friends hanging out and sightseeing, but she was touched York had thought of doing something...more.

She hoped once they were outside again, things would seem more...normal and less...tense.

You can never have too many friends.

His words from last night sounded in her head. She'd lost track of so many or barely kept in touch with others over social media. A new friend would be nice, and she had seen him every day she'd been in Marietta. Being friends could work.

Chantelle had never left a town she'd visited with some-one to call friend. She'd gone in, done her research, and left with only her notes and photographs.

He pulled the key from the ignition. "We have a few minutes to look around."

She slid out of his car. Fresh air filled her lungs. No wor-ries about York being too close, but his standing ten feet away seemed too far.

Pathetic.

Friends didn't worry about space or distance or…

He walked toward her. His movement was athletic, graceful, and confident. "Ever been to a dude ranch?"

"No."

"What do you think?"

I'm glad I'm here with you. That wasn't what he was asking her, but she was acting as if she'd never been around a handsome guy before. Her gaze bounced like a Ping-Pong ball, trying to see everything at once without looking at York until she focused on the building in front of her.

Say something. "I never thought ranches were this high end."

"The Bar V5 pays attention to the details."

As York rocked back on his heels, the sun brought out his golden highlights. He almost looked as if he were wearing a halo. Too funny given his kisses were the definition of temptation.

"Expensive, but worth the money," he said. "They sell out every summer."

Rooftops of smaller guest cabins peeked through the trees in front of where cattle grazed in a pasture. On the other side of the lodge, just beyond the end of the long driveway, was a meadow where horses ran to the fence to greet visitors. Beyond that, she could see other buildings, including an old red barn. The only thing that met her preconceived notions were the sounds of cows and a hint of manure smell mixed in the air, but even that was masked well by the scent of nearby flowers.

She wouldn't mind staying here. The ranch seemed like the perfect place to get away from it all. "They must be doing something right."

York stuck a thumb in his front pocket. "I hope you don't mind this slight detour."

"Not at all." She wanted to experience all Montana had to offer. "I'm glad you suggested we come here."

He motioned to her. "It's almost time."

"For what?"

"You'll see."

His lopsided grin made her catch her breath and sent the butterflies in her stomach flapping. If this kept up, it would be a long afternoon.

Chapter Nine

A MINUTE OR two later, the sound of a motor filled the air. Chantelle looked to her left to see a tractor coming up the driveway. The driver was a blond-haired man—a nice-looking one—wearing a cowboy hat, a western-style shirt, and a navy bandana around his neck.

The tractor pulled a wagon covered in hay. Eli, the cowboy who'd been at the chocolate shop, rode on that.

Even her toes felt as if they were smiling. "We're going on a hayride?"

"Ever been on one?"

"A long time ago when I was little." Chantelle pushed aside the memories. Happy ones, but bittersweet. She didn't want anything to get in the way of her enjoying this. "How did you think of this?"

"I wish I could take credit, but Dustin—he's the one driving—suggested it. There's a bonfire afterward and s'more making."

"Fun." Just as York said.

People climbed onto the wagon with help from Eli and

Dustin. A brown-haired girl dressed completely in pink, including her boots, waved at the cowboys and blew them a kiss, but she didn't get aboard. Chantelle and York moved to a short line that was forming. Soon, it was their turn.

"Welcome to the Bar V5." The blond cowboy was better looking up close, but not as handsome as York. "I'm Dustin."

Earlier, York had told her how Nevada had teamed up with Dustin to up their chances of winning the Valentine Quest in February. Nevada had walked away from the multi-day race with a prize for herself—Dustin.

"Chantelle," she said.

Dustin helped her up into the wagon where Eli was getting everyone seated. "Enjoy the hayride."

As she sat on a hay bale, York took the spot next to her. He'd left space, not quite a foot, between them.

"Do you want me to take your picture?" he asked.

She handed him her phone. "Sure. I can use it on my blog."

"Smile." He held up the camera, snapped it, and then looked closer at the screen. "Cute."

Did he mean the picture or her?

Shouldn't matter.

"Thanks." She took back her phone. "Do you want one?"

"No, thanks." He half-laughed. "If I posted a photo of me doing something fun, even if it's a photo of only me, my mother would start asking me the W-questions."

"W-questions?"

"Who are you with? What's her name? Where did you meet? Why didn't you tell me? Will I get to meet her?"

"Yikes."

"She means well, but she's decided all three of her kids need to settle down ASAP."

"Two out of three…"

"My feelings exactly, but I'm not giving my mom any ammunition." He laughed. "Don't get me wrong. My mom's great, but she's been on this get-married kick for almost a year. It's getting old, but now that Bryce and Dustin are in the picture, I hope she forgets about me.

"I can't imagine anyone forgetting you." The words were out before Chantelle realized what she was saying. Her cheeks burned.

His dark gaze met hers. "Does that mean you'll remember me when you're living in France?"

Not trusting her voice, Chantelle nodded. It wasn't only his kisses that were unforgettable. Something about York himself made him memorable.

He leaned toward her.

Was he going to kiss her?

Heaven help her, but she wanted him to kiss her.

She held her breath. Waited.

York leaned back. "I won't forget you, either."

"Really?" Chantelle wanted to cringe. She sounded like

an insecure teenager.

"Lesley gave Dakota and me each a copy of *The Chocolate Touch* after your book signing, so I'll keep that on my bookcase."

Chantelle's shoulders sagged, and she pushed them back. "When you aren't living out of a suitcase."

"Right. The book will stay at Dakota's until I have a place with a bookcase."

The odds of the book never meeting up with York again sounded high. It shouldn't matter. Chantelle wished she didn't care if he kept the book or not, but a part of her did. She wanted him to remember her. Even if that meant it was remembering the author he'd met and not the time they'd spent together.

She, however, would never forget York Parker. The man, his smile, his kisses. Her feelings about him confused her. The more she tried to figure them out, the more scrambled her thoughts became. It made zero sense. She was the one who'd backed away and jumped at his suggesting they be friends for all the right reasons, yet...

Focus on the future.

Delacroix Chocolates, a place to call home in France, family.

Those three things were what mattered. Nothing else. She forced a friendly smile. "I hope you enjoy the book."

YORK ENJOYED THE hayride. He'd gone all in being Chantelle's friend, and that wasn't working out too bad. He just needed to stop staring at her and inching closer without realizing that was what he was doing. But other than that, he was good.

Chantelle stood next to the bonfire. Flames shot up to the darkening sky. She looked beautiful.

Holding a half-eaten s'more, she glanced his way. "This is the perfect ending to an enjoyable day."

"It is." Watching Chantelle's reactions to the ranch's breathtaking views had been worth the drive.

"I'm so happy you brought me here. It's been great."

"I'm glad."

He wanted to say more, but he pressed his lips together. He was afraid if he started telling her all the reasons he was glad, he would cross over the friend line. Not that telling her what a good sport she'd been when a cow scared her so badly she'd jumped two feet in the air was bad. Or that he was proud of the way she'd overcome her embarrassment when Eli asked her to sing a chorus of a cowboy song he'd taught them. But York wanted to keep himself dialed back.

For both their sakes.

Chantelle crossed her arms over her chest. She wore a light jacket, but the temperature had dropped with the setting sun.

"Are you cold?" he asked.

"A little, but the bonfire is warming me up."

He knew a way to heat her up. Strike that. "Take my

coat."

Shaking her head, she held out her hands toward the fire. "I'm good. Soon, I'll be toasty."

"If not—"

"You don't have to big brother me."

Was that how she saw this? Saw him? "I'm not."

She eyed him warily.

"I brought you here. I don't want you to be miserable." As soon as the words were out, he regretted them. "Or get sick. Or…"

He was making this worse with every word he said.

"That's sweet. I appreciate the concern, but I'm fine." She lowered her hands to her sides. "I'm used to taking care of myself."

I'll take care of you.

The thought sprang out of nowhere.

He took a step away from her because his days of taking care of people were coming to an end. He didn't want anyone else depending on him. He was about to make a fresh start and didn't want to drag any baggage with him.

Oh, he'd always be there for Dakota and Nevada, but they had their boyfriends. The more he got to know Bryce and Dustin, the more he realized how much the men loved his sisters. Neither woman needed York in the same way they once did. That would give him even more freedom come June.

"Goodnight, all," a man with two kids said. The kids

seemed to have more energy than their dad.

Other people remained by the bonfire. A few hearty souls had seconds and thirds of the s'mores.

"Just trying to be a good friend," York said finally.

"You have been." Staring at the bonfire, she stuck her hands in her jacket pocket. "Thanks. And I didn't mean big brother in a negative way. I noticed you talking to Dustin. I figured you were grilling him about his intentions toward Nevada."

"No grilling. The guy makes my baby sister so happy, and the feeling seems mutual," York admitted. "I was just asking him about some of the people in town."

"Clues to narrow down your unsub list?"

"Something like that." York had asked Dustin questions about various residents. Hearing that the judge had changed after a tragedy struck his family made York want to do more for the man, but how could he and keep things secret? "The donor wants to remain anonymous, but I'd still like to do something, however small, so no one on the list would feel singled out."

"What if the donor isn't on your list?" she asked.

The judge wasn't, but only York knew that. "Then I'd be doing random acts of kindness, and I'd hope some paid it forward to include the anonymous benefactor."

"You could say you're doing this to thank the town for sponsoring the event and the residents for supporting it. A quest of your own, except a gratitude one."

"A gratitude quest."

She nodded.

"I like that," he said.

"You really want to thank the person who donated the trip, don't you?"

It was his turn to nod. "According to Dakota, secrets seem to be common knowledge in Marietta, but this one has been hard to crack."

Lines creased Chantelle's forehead. "Secrets should never be shared for public entertainment value. You were the recipient of a fantastic vacation, but if you somehow discover the donor's identity, that isn't your story to tell. Trust whoever it is has a valid reason for remaining anonymous. That's the right—the responsible thing to do. No matter what others in this town might do or say."

"You're right. And thanks."

He wanted to wrap his arms around Chantelle and hug her tight. That was how he saw this, too. Instead, he kept his distance.

"Making this a gratitude quest is a brilliant idea." He could keep the judge's actions a secret but still do something nice for him, as well as for others. A win-win. "I just hope I can pull this off."

She took a breath and then exhaled slowly. "If you need ideas, let me know. I think we're working together on Monday."

"That's Dakota's usual day off."

"Sage mentioned it this morning."

"I haven't heard anything yet."

But York hoped that was the case. Maybe at the chocolate shop, they could go back to the banter and fun they had on Thursday. Friendly fun that would make his wanting to touch and kiss her go away, too.

MONDAY MORNING AT the chocolate shop, Chantelle greeted York with a wave and smile. He'd been on her mind all Sunday. A hundred things she could say swirled through her mind, but she kept her lips pressed together. The same lips that had wished on a star for his kiss on Saturday night. No need to say anything when they'd be working together today.

She headed into the back.

So what if she kept thinking about him?

York was her friend and coworker, nothing more, but women thought about gorgeous guys all the time.

No big deal.

The scent of roasting cacao beans filled the air, and a pot of chocolate was on the stove. She inhaled, letting the aromas soothe her nerves. If only she could stay in the back today…

"Good morning." Sage set out chocolate molds.

Chantelle placed her purse in a cubby before putting on her apron. "Hard at work already."

"I like to start early."

Chantelle spent yesterday working on her report about Copper Mountain Chocolates and still had a couple of questions. Might as well get the answers before the shop officially opened. "Do you start early so you can leave early?"

"Yes. I like to be out of here before school gets out, and I try to limit the Saturdays I work."

"That must work out well with the kids."

"Better than I expected it would." Sage checked the contents in the pot. "I opened the shop before I was married. Back then, Copper Mountain Chocolates was my only baby, but with some juggling and a helpful husband, owning a business and being a mom has worked out well."

The chocolatier didn't sound unhappy or frustrated, like someone who wanted out of an overwhelming situation. If anything, her tone spoke of being content and in control. That was good for Sage, but not for Uncle Laurent if he wanted Copper Mountain Chocolates.

"Must be tiring doing it all," Chantelle said.

"It's a constant state." Sage laughed. Her smile lit up her face. "Though I think the tiredness is more due to being a mom than anything else. Family life is crazy busy, but Savannah and Braden are the best kids. I wouldn't change anything."

"Not even the hours you have to work?"

As Sage tilted her head, a satisfied smile graced her lips. "Nope, everything is great. Of course, I wouldn't complain if I had an extra hour to spend with my husband, but who wouldn't?"

Chantelle agreed. "I'd take the extra hour in my day, and I don't even have a boyfriend or family around."

"The more people in your life, the less time you'll have, but being surrounded by loved ones is worth it. Even when things don't work out quite as planned."

"Portia in the hospital?"

Sage nodded. "I was hoping my niece would have an easier time, but as long as the little one stays put for another week or two, things should be fine."

Chantelle looked forward to having people—family—around her. "Do you need any help back here?"

"No, thanks." Sage lowered the heat on the stovetop. "I don't think I mentioned it on Saturday, but I make all the chocolate. The staff works out front and helps with packaging products."

Chantelle had heard that at the tasting, but she'd wanted to confirm the information. "That's a lot of work for one person."

"It's my way of ensuring quality control."

"Does that include the hot chocolate?" Chantelle asked.

Sage nodded. "Everything we sell, I make."

"Well, have fun back here." That was the final piece of information Chantelle needed, but it wasn't what she'd hoped to hear for her uncle's sake. "I'd better get out front and see if York needs help."

"Thanks again for filling in for Portia."

"Happy to help." Chantelle walked out into the front and joined York behind the display case. He wore the same uniform as he had on Thursday and Friday, but something about him seemed different this morning. His smile was brighter or maybe the color of his eyes was deeper. Whatever it was, he looked great, more handsome than before.

"Ready for another day of chocolate?" he asked.

"Of course." She only hoped she stopped noticing things about him.

"Did you do anything fun yesterday?" he asked.

"I walked to the park, ate at the Main Street Diner, and then worked."

"The first two sound like fun. The third, not so much."

"Haven't you heard that saying about loving what you do and it not feeling like work?"

"Yes, and I love working with computers, but it can still feel like work."

She double-checked the plate of samples to make sure a pair of silver tongs were nearby. "You have a point, but writing the review about this place was fun. How was your Sunday?"

"My sisters and I went to Bozeman. I'd mentioned the gratitude quest, and they wanted to help."

A heaviness pressed down on Chantelle's shoulders. She bent her neck forward, ignoring the unexpected disappointment that he hadn't needed her help. She tried to shake it off. "That must have been fun."

"It was. We're each doing things for people." York's eyes sparkled with excitement. "This morning, Dakota's delivering cookies and muffins to the staff at the Copper Mountain Animal Hospital, and a cheesecake to Tim, the owner of Paradise Valley Feed Store. Both places have partnered with the animal rescue where she volunteers. Nevada is doing hers later. It's coming to the end of the term at the university so she has to finish up grading for her class."

The only random act of kindness Chantelle had ever done was paying for someone's coffee order in the drive-thru line. She liked the idea of doing more. "I'd like to join in the gratitude quest."

"You would?"

She nodded. "This is important to you."

A beat passed. And another. "It is. Thanks."

His gaze held hers. Whatever connection had passed between them before was back and stronger than before.

Something fluttered in her stomach. A tingle turned into two, and then into more than she could count.

Look away.

But she couldn't.

The bell on the door jingled.

York broke eye contact. "Welcome to Copper Mountain Chocolates."

Chantelle should be relieved someone had entered the shop when they did, but a part of her was disappointed. Again.

She forced at smile at the two women entering the store. Both went to the back wall where copper boxes of chocolates were displayed.

"I'll help them," York said. He walked over to the customers.

Chantelle nodded. She was grateful for the distance.

Being around York made it hard to think straight. That had never been an issue before with any man she'd dated, and it worried her. Maybe sticking around town after she sent off her report wasn't the best idea, even if Sage did need the extra help right now. Chantelle couldn't let anything interfere with her plans, especially a good-looking former air force captain who could turn her into a pile of mush with a simple smile.

BEING JUST FRIENDS *sucked.*

Clearing off a table, York forced himself not to look at Chantelle as she rang up a cowboy's order. This was the second time the guy had been in this morning. Guess the hot chocolate during his first visit hadn't been enough.

Chantelle laughed.

York's shoulder muscles bunched. He shouldn't look, but he did.

The guy was leaning over the counter toward Chantelle. Whatever he was saying had brought a blush to her cheeks.

It shouldn't matter, but it did.

Maybe by the time York carried the dirty dishes to the

back, the guy would be gone. He didn't want to make a scene, but he'd feel the same way if it were Dakota behind the counter.

He dumped the dishes in the back and went out front.

The cowboy was still standing there. His order had been paid and he held the bag, but that didn't stop him from grinning and chatting up Chantelle in his faded jeans, boots, and too-tight T-shirt as if this were a pickup joint.

"Do you work here every day?" the cowboy asked. Even though this was Montana, he spoke with a Southern twang. Obviously fake.

Chantelle shook her head. "It just depends on when I'm scheduled."

The guy kept staring at her. No blinking. Talk about weird. "You ever go to Grey's?"

"I've been once," she said.

With me, York wanted to say, but he didn't. He did recognize the help-me-please glance she shot his way.

He hadn't wanted to interfere, but now that he had an invitation, he walked behind the counter, stood next to Chantelle, and crossed his arms over his chest.

The cowboy rocked back on his heels. "I'll be there tonight if you want to drop by. Tomorrow's my day off so I can stay up late. All night, even."

Way to go with being subtle, bozo.

York was finished with the clown. "The dishes are ready to be washed."

"I'll get right on that." She glanced at the cowboy, but her smile looked pasted on, not real. "Have a nice day."

"See you at Grey's," the cowboy said.

As Chantelle walked into the back, the cowboy's gaze zeroed in on her butt. "Now that's one fine piece of—"

"Do you need anything else?"

"Other than her?" The man's smirk made York's hands fist. "No."

Don't lose it. This wasn't a bar. Chantelle wasn't interested. The guy was a loser.

Taking a deep breath, York flexed his fingers. "Enjoy your chocolates."

The cowboy took one more look toward the back before swaggering out the door.

"He's gone," York said.

Chantelle walked out. "Thank goodness. I didn't think he was going to leave. He was so friendly and funny this morning, but when he came back, the more he said, the more uncomfortable I was."

She shivered.

York touched her arm. Heat radiated from the point of contact and pulsed up his hand.

"You okay now?" He forced the words from his dry throat.

She nodded. "I'm going to stay away from Grey's."

"Excellent idea," he agreed. "Though if you really want to go, I can be your bodyguard."

She laughed. "You've had the perfect training."

"What?"

"Two younger sisters."

He laughed. "Right."

Chantelle smiled up at him and sent a bunch of butter-flies loose in his gut. "Thank you."

"Happy to help."

"I know you are, and I'm happy to be the recipient." Her gaze softened. "It's only Monday morning, and you've accomplished a good deed for your gratitude quest."

Emotion clogged his throat. What he'd done had nothing to do with the gratitude quest. He'd been angry and…jealous.

But no matter how attractive he found Chantelle, he wouldn't stoop to the cowboy's level. He'd find a way to deal with his attraction…his desire for her.

Or drive himself crazy trying.

SOMEHOW, CHANTELLE SURVIVED working all day with York despite her growing awareness of him. When he'd stepped in to save her from the flirty cowboy, she'd wanted to kiss him.

Who was she kidding?

She wanted to kiss him each time she saw him.

When she'd dropped a pair of silver tongs, they'd both got down on the floor only to find themselves face to face, so close together his breath caressed her cheek. For the second time that day, she thought he might kiss her, but the sound of Sage's voice had broken whatever spell they'd been under.

His knight-in-shining-armor save this morning had only deepened her feelings for him. With an exasperated sigh, she plopped onto the bed in her room at the Graff.

Stop thinking about York Parker.

The report was waiting to be finished. She wanted to send that off tonight. And would.

If she could get her thoughts under control.

Sitting cross-legged on the bed, she went to work—adding details she'd wanted to clarify and proofing the document. Next, she wrote the conclusion.

Copper Mountain Chocolates has created delicious and highly respectable products that fulfill its niche market in a western tourist town. In addition to her quality chocolate, Sage Carrigan O'Dell has built a welcoming shop with a loyal clientele. The family atmosphere and monthly events draw in customers. Shuttering the shop would be detrimental to the community at large. A merchandising agreement would not make up for the loss of sales that would occur at the shop since that is part of the appeal to customers, both regulars and tourists. The experience of visiting the shop is as much a draw as the products themselves.

The Criollo Bar stands out among the shop's offerings and would add another option to Delacroix's chocolate bars. However, that collection continues to gain market share, so an analysis would be required as to the acquisition cost versus profit estimation.

Based on my interactions with the staff, Mrs. O'Dell gives no indication of wanting to sell her business. I don't know how receptive she will be to a purchase offer. She is a hands-on owner who produces all her own products. Employees are not involved in any step of the process or creation of chocolates or hot chocolate. Employees have no access to recipes or knowledge of how products are made. This suggests the lack of a contingency or emergency plan should Mrs. O'Dell become sick or injured. That is the only scenario where I imagine an offer being welcome and/or accepted.

Although Copper Mountain Chocolates is a successful small batch producer with traditional offerings and fresh spins on old favorites, my recommendation is to not pursue. I believe the time and effort of putting together a purchase agreement would be a waste of Delacroix's legal and financial resources.

After saving the document, she slumped against the bed's headboard. This wasn't what she'd hoped to write after tasting the delicious chocolate last week, nor was it what her uncle hoped to hear, but she had to be honest. Her research and her gut told her Sage would not be open to selling her recipes and closing Copper Mountain Chocolates, so why should Delacroix Chocolates spend money on the effort?

Sure, most people had a price, but Chantelle had a feeling Sage's would be so high the deal wouldn't make financial sense.

There was something else, too.

Chantelle didn't want the chocolate shop to go away. She'd only worked a few shifts, and barely knew the staff, but she loved what she'd experienced so far at Copper Mountain Chocolates.

Each hour she'd spent there had opened her eyes to what making and selling chocolates was all about. She enjoyed the customer interaction and seeing how they decided what to order. The welcoming feel made the shop a homey place to go.

Not that any of that would matter to Uncle Laurent.

He would make the final decision, and she hoped she'd given him enough information to do so. One that would be in the best interest of Delacroix Chocolates.

Her recommendation was only her opinion. Philippe, who dealt with numbers, might disagree with her assessment or be able to come up with a purchase offer that would sway Sage and allow a return on their investment.

Chantelle tapped send.

Her evening was now free. She could eat, check out more shops, or see a movie, but staying in her room appealed to her the most.

A knock sounded. "Concierge."

Chantelle opened the door.

A woman dressed in a blue jacket and skirt handed her a pastel-colored floral gift bag. "This was left for you. If there's anything I can do for you, Ms. Cummings, please don't hesitate to ask."

"Thanks." Chantelle carried the bag to the bed. Tucked inside the tissue paper was an envelope. She opened it.

Thanks for suggesting the Gratitude Quest, Chantelle.
York

How sweet of him. She'd never expected to be included.

Excited, Chantelle removed the pink and yellow sheets of tissue paper, then pulled out a Criollo bar from the chocolate shop. She laughed. He knew what her favorite item was.

Next came a cellophane bag of cookies from the Copper Mountain Gingerbread and Dessert Factory. They'd peered through the bakery's window on Saturday but hadn't had enough time to go inside. The final item was a book—a thick paperback travel guide about France.

Heat balled at the center of her chest and radiated outward. Whatever weight she'd felt pressing down on her before disappeared. She felt light, as if she were about to float away, and clutched the book to weigh her down.

An image of York formed in her mind.

Such a kind and caring man.

This gift might be a random act of kindness, but York had put thought into each item. She'd never been so…touched.

She'd told him earlier she wanted to join in the gratitude quest, but she hadn't thought about it more than that with the report due.

Now she could.

She would make something for York, Lesley the bookstore owner, and for Walt. Anyone who thought chocolate should be a food group deserved a little present. Chantelle would also give something to each of the staff at Copper Mountain Chocolates.

And she knew what one of the items would be. She'd make one of her mother's chocolate recipes.

Chantelle tapped her chin. She'd need to find a kitchen to use. Nothing fancy, a stove and counter space. Asking Sage to use the shop to make chocolate like this didn't feel right. Maybe Dakota wouldn't mind. Chantelle would ask York.

But she wouldn't tell him that some of what she would be making would be his. She smiled. He'd figure that out when he got the rest of his gifts.

ON WEDNESDAY, YORK unlocked the front door to Dakota's house. Behind him, Chantelle held onto grocery bags. Yesterday, she'd asked if she could use the kitchen. He'd said yes without asking his sister. He knew she wouldn't care.

He opened the door.

Fang's barks filled the air.

"Someone doesn't sound happy," Chantelle said.

He glanced over his shoulder. She wore a pretty pink cardigan sweater that was buttoned up to the top with a pair of black jeans.

"Fang wants out of his crate. He's an older dog. Not too rambunctious, but he'll need to wind down a little. Do you mind?"

"Not at all."

York motioned Chantelle inside. "Let's get you settled in the kitchen before I release the hound."

As she walked past, her vanilla scent made him want to take another sniff.

"Are your sisters home?" she asked.

"No." He closed the front door. Fang's barks turned to whines. "Dakota is having dinner at Walt's, and Nevada is out at the Bar V5 with Dustin. The kitchen is all yours."

"I appreciate this."

She'd said something similar about his gratitude gifts to her. Her smile and sparkling eyes had been the only thank you he needed, then and now. "Not a problem."

Inside the house, he pointed to the hallway that led to the kitchen at the back.

"Why do you need a kitchen?" he asked.

"I want to make something for my gratitude gifts."

She'd told him she was joining in, so he shouldn't be surprised, but he didn't understand why she was doing it. She had no connection to Marietta or the people who lived here. "I hope you don't feel obligated."

"I don't have to do this, but I want to. That's the point of the gratitude quest. Random acts. No reason required."

She had a point.

"True." Except for Judge Kingsley. "What are you going to make?"

Chantelle switched one of the bags she was holding to her other hand. "You'll see."

"Is it a surprise?"

"Not really. More of a mystery. You like those, right?"

"I do. Will I get a taste?"

"Do you want one?" She entered the kitchen.

"Yes." He was curious what she might make.

Zip, the small black foster cat, darted between his legs as if running an obstacle course or trying to trip him. The cat headed toward Chantelle.

"Watch out for the cat," York said.

She glanced down. The cat rubbed against her pant leg. "You are a cutie."

"Very cute, but I haven't decided if Zip has a death wish or is the mastermind of a superhero archenemy."

Chantelle emptied her bags onto the table. Two bags of chocolate chips, a carton of cream, a jar of honey, cocoa powder, and something he didn't recognize. A spice, maybe?

The names on the bags didn't match the stores in Marietta. "Where did you go shopping?"

"Bozeman." She removed small white boxes stacked inside one another, a mesh sieve, a set of wooden spoons, a large glass measuring cup, a small ice cream scooper, and a roll of parchment paper. "I needed a craft store."

"You went to a lot of trouble."

She shrugged.

He picked up one of the bags of chocolate chips. It was bittersweet and the other milk chocolate. "Are you making some kind of chocolate?"

She nodded once.

"I'm sure Sage would give you a discount. You don't have to make something yourself."

"I don't have to, but I want to. I love making chocolates, and I rarely get the chance. Doing this is a real treat."

"*The Chocolate Touch* extends beyond writing about chocolate?"

"Way beyond. There are a few recipes in the book."

His face heated. He hadn't looked at the book beyond the front and back covers.

"It's okay if you didn't know that."

He would look through the book tonight. "What else do you need?"

"Do you have a saucepan, bowl, and cookie sheet?"

"Coming right up." He removed those from the cupboards and placed them on the counter. "Anything else?"

Chantelle washed her hands. "That's it. Thanks."

"I'm going to get Fang and let him into the backyard. He usually uses the door back here, but I'm going to take him around front to the gate. Otherwise, he'll be all over you. Be right back."

"I'll be here."

York made it as far as the doorway before glancing over his shoulder. "Your sweater is really nice. Do you want to borrow a shirt so it doesn't get dirty?"

"I didn't think about that, but I have a shirt on underneath." She unbuttoned her sweater. "Thanks, though, I should know how messy chocolate can be."

"Which is why we wear aprons at the shop."

He was glad Chantelle wasn't wearing one and covering her pale pink T-shirt that stretched across her chest.

York tugged at his now-too-tight collar. He was supposed to be doing something, but he couldn't remember what that was.

A bark sounded.

Fang.

He walked into the living room and grabbed a leash. "Sorry, boy." York kept his voice low. "I was distracted."

Fang's brown eyes stared up at him.

"You'll see when you meet her, but first you're going to the backyard."

The dog's tail wagged.

When York returned to the kitchen, a delicious aroma filled the air.

"Something smells good," he said.

She stirred whatever was inside the saucepan. A contented smile was on her face. "I hope it tastes as good."

York didn't care how it tasted. Watching her was enough. The passion in her eyes reminded him of how she looked during the chocolate tasting.

He leaned against the counter. "You're enjoying yourself."

She nodded. "My mom taught me about chocolate. When I make something, I think about all those times we spent together in the kitchen. The memories are so good."

"You should be a chocolatier so you are always making chocolate."

A wistful expression crossed her face. "That would be a dream job."

"Go for it."

Her mouth quirked. "You haven't tried anything I've made."

"No, but you have the chocolate touch, right?"

He expected her to laugh, but her gaze clouded instead. She didn't say anything.

"What?" he asked.

"My book title came from something my mom told me when I was little. She said everyone born into her family has the chocolate touch, including me. I never quite believed it, but I still hope…"

The vulnerability in her voice made him want to reach out to her. "Believe, Chantelle. When you're around chocolate or talking about chocolate, there's something different about you. A passion. Joy."

"That's sweet of you."

"Not sweet. True." York walked to the stove. He was drawn to her in a way he couldn't explain, but he didn't care. "Chantelle, I…"

Her lips parted slightly.

He brushed his mouth over hers.

"I know I mentioned being friends, but I have to be honest," York said. "That's not enough for me. You're beautiful, smart, funny, and so many other things. I've been fighting this attraction, and it's a losing battle. I'm ready to surrender."

"Me, too. I was ready a couple of days ago."

"I just need to make sure no matter what happens with us, it won't influence or change your feelings about Copper Mountain Chocolates."

"It won't. That's not how I work. I promise."

"Great." That was what he needed to hear. "What do you want to do now?"

"Besides kiss?"

He laughed. "Kissing is a given."

She stared up at him through her eyelashes. The battle between the shyness and daring in her gaze was intoxicating.

"What if we don't put too much thought into this and just spend time together as long as we're in Marietta?" she asked.

Neither of them were in a position for something long

term, but he hadn't expected her to say that. "I'd like that."

"Me, too."

Her tongue swept across her lower lip in a sexy move that made him lean in to kiss her again. This time, he let his lips linger and enjoyed her sweet taste. His arms went around her to pull her against him.

She arched to bring herself closer.

Heat pulsed through him, and an ache grew.

One kiss would never satisfy his hunger for her. She pressed her mouth against his with the same desire he felt.

From a spark to a flame to an inferno.

His hands dug into her hair, the silky strands sifting through his fingers.

He wanted more…all of her.

She backed away. "If I don't stir the cream, it'll burn."

He was burning up himself.

"Can I take a raincheck on the kisses?" she asked.

Chantelle didn't act freaked out or overwhelmed. She looked like a woman who'd been kissed and wanted more.

He was happy to oblige. "You can have as many rainchecks as you'd like."

Her eyes danced. "Then I'd like at least a dozen."

York had no idea what he was doing. He didn't want a relationship. A steady girlfriend was the last thing he needed. If she traveled as much as he did, they'd never be able to see each other. But this woman next to him was special, and he wanted to spend time with her while he had the opportunity.

They could figure out the rest, even if that just meant saying goodbye and not looking back when the time came to leave Marietta.

With a smile, he stepped away from the stove so she'd have more room. "That can be arranged."

Chapter Ten

THE NEXT MORNING, Chantelle stretched in her bed. She hadn't stopped smiling since spending the evening in Dakota's kitchen, making chocolates and kissing York. She had no idea what would happen with him, but she was okay with that.

For now, at least.

Being with York made her happy. Yes, she could be making a huge mistake by being more than friends. Her goal was to have a serious, long-term relationship, but she wasn't in town that long.

A few kisses and fun times together didn't mean she and York were compatible or would want to date beyond the next week or two. Why not make the most of the time she had with him? If she remained focused on her goals—moving to France to be closer to her family and working at Delacroix Chocolates–she would be fine.

Her cell phone rang.

Was it York?

She grabbed her phone. A name flashed on the screen.

Philippe.

Oh, well… Chantelle answered the call. "Hello."

"Good morning." Philippe sounded cheery. "I hope I didn't wake you."

"I'm up and ready to start my day."

"Are you working at the shop today?"

"No." She thought about York's invitation when he'd said goodnight. "I'm going out to breakfast. After that, I have a radio interview about the book."

"You sound happier than usual."

She hadn't expected Philippe to notice, but she was pleased he had.

"I am." Chantelle wanted to be upfront with her cousin. That was what family did with one another. At least, she hoped so. "I met someone. We're meeting for breakfast."

"Is he from Marietta?"

"No. York is just in town visiting his sisters this month. He's working a few shifts at the chocolate shop. That's how we got to know each other."

"An office romance," her cousin teased.

"Sort of." She hadn't thought about it like that. "Though a shop romance might be a better description. But I'm sure you didn't call to hear about my social life."

"No, but I like knowing what's going on with you."

That made her smile. Philippe, on the other hand, was easy to keep track of. Her cousin was either at work or asleep. She often wondered if he slept in his office.

"What's up?" she asked.

"Father and I went over your report."

Chantelle gripped the phone tighter.

"I analyzed our chocolate bars by individual flavor and collection sales as you suggested," Philippe continued. "Good call on passing. Father has decided to follow your recommendation and not pursue Copper Mountain Chocolates. We don't need their Criollo bar, though it sounds delicious."

She released her breath. "A wise decision."

Not only because that was the right decision for Delacroix Chocolates, but also for her Copper Mountain Chocolate coworkers and their customers. Not to mention the town of Marietta.

"Thanks for giving us the information we needed," Philippe said. "When will you be returning to Boston?"

"I'm not sure. My schedule is flexible, but I've been thinking of extending my stay."

"Is York the reason you want to stay longer?"

Philippe had remembered York's name. "We've been hanging out, but I'll be helping at the chocolate shop until their other employee returns from her vacation."

"You're gaining invaluable experience."

"I'm learning so much about selling chocolate and customer service," she admitted. "I'm also loving Marietta. There's this gratitude thing going on that's wonderful. People are doing random acts of kindness for others around town. So many are joining in after receiving something or hearing about it. Last night, I made lavender-infused truffles to give away. York said they were as good as what Sage makes. Though he's biased."

"If your truffles are half as good as what you made Father and me when you were here, they must be outstanding."

Philippe's words gave Chantelle a boost of confidence. "Thanks."

"It's true, but you need to believe it."

York had said something similar last night, but she was so afraid she wouldn't fit in with her family in France when she wanted to. Desperately. "I'm trying."

"Try harder." Silence filled the line. "I have a meeting before I head home, and you need to get ready for your breakfast date. Let me know how it goes."

"You care?"

"I do, Chantelle. I know we haven't spent much time together in person, but I enjoy our conversations. You are family, and the closest thing I have to a sister."

Joy overflowed. "Thank you, Philippe. I always wanted a brother."

Her dreams seemed to be coming true. Well, all but a happily ever after. She knew York wasn't her forever love, but she could see him as her prince charming for now. That was better than nothing.

HAVING BREAKFAST WITH Chantelle at the Main Street Diner was the perfect way to start the day. York held her hand across the table. His leg touched hers beneath it.

She raised her orange juice. "The food is excellent."

Not as tasty as her kisses. York smiled as he remembered saying goodnight. "It's one of my favorites in town."

"I'm still partial to Rocco's."

"Another favorite."

She stared over the rim of her glass. "You have a few favorites."

He shrugged. "Being with you makes them more special."

"You have a way with words." She took another sip.

"Not words, the truth." He finished the coffee in his cup. "I found a gift bag with my name on it after you left."

If she was trying to keep her face neutral, she was failing. Big time.

"Oh, really?" she asked.

"You should have seen what was inside." He counted off on his fingers. "A pocket map of the US so I can mark off where I travel, a mini flu and cold kit with everything I might need if I get sick on the road, a pamphlet on how to tie a bow, and a box of truffles that look like the ones you made last night. I loved everything. Thank you."

Her smile brightened her face. "You're welcome."

"Don't doubt if you were born with the chocolate touch or not. You were." He raised her hand to his mouth and kissed the top. "Those truffles were amazing. My sisters loved their boxes of chocolates, too."

"I'm glad."

He kissed her hand again. "This gratitude quest has turned out even better than I expected."

Her gaze locked on his. "I can say the same thing about my trip to Marietta. It's turned out much differently, been much sweeter, than I expected. Because of you."

Her words hit his heart like an arrow. York wanted to spend as much time with her as he could. "How long are you staying in town?"

"My cousin was asking me that same question this morning since I was supposed to fly home yesterday."

"I'm here until the end of the month."

"You mentioned that."

He still had no idea how this was going to work out, but it was looking good so far. "You should extend your stay for a couple of weeks."

"I'll think about it."

The server placed a black leather bill folder on the table, and York reached for it. "Thanks."

A few minutes later, he walked out of the café with Chantelle. "Do you have anything going on this morning?"

"A phone interview with a radio station in Boise, Idaho. You?"

"I need to deliver one of my gratitude gifts this morning."

"Who's this one for?"

"Judge Kingsley. He lives in that old, rundown house on Bramble Lane."

"Excellent choice for your gratitude quest."

York thought so, but for different reasons than Chantelle's. "Dustin told me a few things about the judge. I've never met him, but as you said, that's the whole point of random acts."

"You're the sweetest." She kissed York's cheek. "I need to get back to the hotel. Can we meet up later?"

"I'll be working this afternoon with Dakota, but I'm free after that."

"Text or call me."

"I will." He kissed her on the lips. "Good luck with your interview."

"Have fun making your delivery."

York watched her walk down the street toward the direction of her hotel. He hoped she extended her stay until the end of the month.

Five minutes later, York stood in front of the neglected house that belonged to Judge Kingsley. Overgrown shrubs and large, untrimmed trees hid much of the house. Broken branches lay in the yard of patchy brown grass. Dead plants were everywhere.

Why would anyone want to live here?

The place looked decrepit.

He walked up to the front door with a gift bag in hand.

Inside were a box of Copper Mountain Chocolates, a decorated bottle that contained sand from Fiji, a Legal Decisions paperweight, cat toys and treats, and a handheld electronic game.

Something hissed from behind a bush. That must be the guard cat that Dustin had mentioned. That was why York had picked up a few cat items for the gift bag.

The hisses turned to growls.

York wasn't deterred. He went to the front door and knocked.

No answer.

The cat screeched.

He knocked again.

"Go away," a grouchy male voice said from behind the closed door.

The judge had the reputation of being the meanest man in town, and so far, he was living up to that. York knew better. Like the still-growling cat, the judge's bark was for show only.

"Hello," York said. "I have something for Judge Kingsley. It's part of a gratitude quest that's going on around town."

"A what?"

"A gratitude quest," York repeated. "It's my way to thank the community for putting on the Valentine Quest."

"I had nothing to with that."

Sure, he didn't. York smiled. "That's fine. It's not necessary that you were involved. This a random-acts-of-kindness sort of thing. You live in Marietta, so you're included."

The judge harrumphed. "I agree on the random, but I've heard something like this has been going on."

"It's catching on with more and more people."

The door cracked open. Only an inch, but York would take that.

"Did you start it?" the judge asked.

"A friend came up with the idea, and then I ran with it."

"Who are you?"

"York Parker. I was the recipient of the grand prize won by Dustin Decker."

The door opened another quarter of an inch, but York couldn't see the judge. Just his shadow.

"Did you enjoy yourself?" Judge Kingsley asked.

"I did, thank you." *There!* York had said the two words he wanted to say. "It was exactly the vacation I needed, so much fun, and to top it off, my friend who went along with me met the woman of his dreams there."

York held out the gift bag. "This is for you. There's something for your cat, too."

The judge didn't say anything, nor did the crack widen further.

Stalemate.

That was okay. York hadn't expected to speak with the man given what Dustin had said, so this would do.

"I've taken enough of your time, sir." York set the gift

bag in front of the crack. "I'll leave this for you and your cat. Have a nice day."

York heard the door open more, but he didn't glance back. He kept walking. Each step brought more yowls from the cat. He didn't care. He'd done what he came to do—say thank you to the judge.

That deserved a celebration tonight with Chantelle. She was part French. A bottle of bubbly might go over well.

Forget going to Grey's.

Only the Graff would do tonight.

FROM DRINKING CHAMPAGNE at the Graff to watching a matinee at the local theater when neither of them had to work, each day that week brought something new to experience with York. He was still doing things with his sisters, but he made time for Chantelle every day.

Dates and kisses. Kisses and dates. Oh, and chocolate. She'd never been happier.

On Friday, she arrived at the shop and went to the back to put away her purse. Sage was standing near the roaster.

"Good morning." Chantelle tied on her apron.

"Same to you. I heard from Rosie last night," Sage said. "She'll be back in town next week, so Monday will be your last shift here. You've been an immense help, but I'm sure you must be ready to go home."

Chantelle's one-bedroom apartment in Boston was as

much a home as her room at the Graff Hotel. If anything, this shop had become her home. But that was ending.

Whatever she had with York would be over, too. The only question left was whether she should leave Marietta next week or wait until the end of the month when York left. Either way, he wouldn't be a part of her life for much longer. He wouldn't be there to put a smile on her face, make her laugh, or kiss her until she went weak in the knees. He'd shown her how much she'd been missing in her life these past three years. She didn't want to lose that.

Or him.

A lump burned in her throat. She forced a smile. "Thanks. This has been fun, but I'm sure you're ready to have your regular staff back."

"By the way," Sage said. "I tried one of your lavender-infused chocolate truffles. Delicious."

"Thanks. It was one of my mom's recipes."

Maybe York was correct. Maybe Chantelle had the skills to do great things at Delacroix Chocolates.

AFTER CHANTELLE WORKED at the chocolate shop, York walked her to the Graff. The last thing he wanted was a girlfriend, but if he was in the market, she'd be the woman for him. Fun, didn't ask the typical relationship questions, kissed like a dream, and understood about his family obligations.

Even on a Friday night.

"You're sure you don't mind?" he asked.

"Go have dinner with your sisters," Chantelle said. "Dakota and Nevada are the reasons you're in Marietta. Family time is important."

"You're important to me, too."

"Aw, thanks. But I'll be fine."

Chantelle was saying all the right things, but her smile didn't quite reach her eyes. Maybe she was tired from her shift. "You need to eat."

"I will."

"I'll call you when I'm done, and we can do something."

"I'd like that a lot." She kissed him. "Have fun with your sisters."

A little while later, York slid into a large booth at the pizza parlor. Next to him were Nevada and Dustin. On the other side were Dakota, Bryce, and Walt.

"Sorry I'm late." York hadn't realized everyone would be here. "I didn't leave the chocolate shop right at five."

Bryce poured him a beer from a pitcher.

Mischief filled Walt's eyes. "Were you working with Chantelle today?"

York nodded.

"She can make a whipped cream tower almost as good as Dakota," Nevada said.

"Almost is the key word." Dakota laughed. "I will say Chantelle's truffles were amazing. It's too bad Monday is her last day helping out at the shop."

York straightened. "What do you mean?"

"Rosie called. She'll be back on Monday night," Dakota said. "She and her brother worked hard when she was in LA, so she now has extra time to fill in while Portia is on maternity leave."

Why hadn't Chantelle told him? Not that it mattered if she were helping at the shop or not. She could still stay in Marietta until the end of the month to spend time with him.

"Does that mean my shifts will be cut, too?" York asked.

"Yes, you need time off so you don't spend your entire vacation working."

"Sounds good to me." He would rather spend it with Chantelle.

As the talk shifted to Walt's most recent card game night, York noticed the noise level rising in the pizza parlor. A line had formed in front of the takeout counter that went out the door.

A blonde caught his eyes.

He did a double-take.

Chantelle.

Guilt coated his throat, but he didn't understand why. She wasn't his girlfriend or anything. They were just hanging out and spending time together. He'd done nothing wrong. He was supposed to have dinner with his sisters, which he was doing. It wasn't his fault they'd invited others to join them.

But he hadn't.

The thought of including Chantelle had never crossed his mind. That didn't mean he should feel bad because he hadn't invited her. He wasn't dating her the way his sisters were dating their boyfriends.

Besides, the last thing he needed was one of his sisters mentioning Chantelle to their mom. Her meddling would only get worse. No way would he give Mom ammunition.

Chantelle paid for her pizza, turned, and walked to the door.

Walt waved at her. "Chantelle."

Smiling, she waved back. Her gaze met York's for a second, but that was enough to make him feel like a complete jerk. He watched her leave.

Walt shook his head. "Hard to believe a pretty woman like that will be eating pizza alone in her hotel room."

"Dad," Bryce warned. "You promised. No more playing matchmaker."

Walt held up his hands, palms facing out. "Just making a statement."

Nevada and Dakota laughed.

Dustin looked like he was about to join in, but then he picked up his beer and took a long drink.

That seemed like the best course of action to York. He did the same.

No reason to feel weird, he told himself. She'd been the one to tell him to go out tonight. It wasn't like they were in a relationship, one that was deep with feeling involved.

By the time the pizza arrived, York had lost his appetite. He wanted dinner to be over so he could see Chantelle. He didn't know if he owed her an explanation or an apology, but he needed to make sure she was okay.

Maybe he was feeling this way because he knew they wouldn't be working together at the shop. Something was making him feel weird.

York tapped his foot, but that didn't make anyone eat faster. By the time the bill arrived, he was ready to go.

"Who's up for Grey's?" Dustin asked.

"Me," Nevada said.

Bryce nodded. "I'm game."

"Where you go, I go." Dakota held Bryce's hand.

"Thanks, but I'm heading home," Walt said. "Big bridge tournament tomorrow. I need my beauty sleep."

"York?" Nevada asked.

"I need to make a phone call, and then I'll meet you over there." He would invite Chantelle to join them. Maybe this weirdness inside him would go away, then.

As soon as the others were out of sight, he crossed Front Avenue and entered the Graff Hotel. He called Chantelle from the lobby.

One ring. Two rings. Three…

"Hello."

"Hey," he said. "I'm finished with dinner. My sisters didn't tell me they were inviting the others. I didn't mean to exclude you."

Silence.

Not a good sign.

"Do your sisters know we've been…whatever you'd call what we've been doing?" Chantelle asked.

He hesitated. "They know we're friends and hang out."

"Friends."

Sweat dampened the back of his neck. He felt on the defensive, but he wasn't sure why. One of the reasons he didn't want a girlfriend was to avoid situations like these. So why was he feeling this way with Chantelle?

"I haven't said more because I don't want my mom going crazy if she hears anything from my sisters," he explained.

That had sounded like a good excuse when he'd thought of it, but once he'd said the words, not so much.

"Everyone except Walt is on their way to Grey's," he added. "Come with me."

That invitation should make everything better.

"Thanks, but I just got off the phone with my cousin and am in my pajamas. I'm going to bed early."

Her cousin who lived in France? That meant a middle-of-the-night call for him. Not good.

York's throat clogged. "I'm sorry if I hurt your feelings."

"I just need to figure a few things out." Her voice was so soft he had to strain to hear her. "I think it's time for me to go."

That wasn't what he expected to hear. A good thing he hadn't eaten much because his stomach was churning. "Why?"

"Rosie Linn is coming back. Sage doesn't need my help."

"What about…" He almost said *us*, but that wasn't the right word. There was no *us* or *we*. They weren't a couple. At least, that wasn't what he'd planned on happening when this started. "I thought you were going to stay until the end of the month. That way we'd have more time together."

"Is that what you want?"

"Yes." He didn't hesitate.

"I don't know." She sounded—not exactly sad, but maybe defeated. "I'm not sure I can keep doing what we've been doing."

"What do you mean?" he asked.

"Seeing you tonight with everyone made me feel left out. Except I realize I had no reason to feel that way. I'm not your girlfriend. I'm just someone you're spending time with for a couple of weeks, so it makes sense I wouldn't be included in family stuff. I shouldn't have felt excluded because I wasn't invited, but since I did, maybe it is better not to get more involved."

"I understand." Even if he didn't like it. She'd mentioned wanting to be closer to family because she had none here in the States. No wonder she felt excluded. That was probably how she felt most of the time. "I felt like a jerk when I saw you tonight."

"Thanks for saying that."

At least he'd done something right. But the truth was if he didn't care about her, he wouldn't feel so bad over what happened. "You're more than someone I'm just spending time with for a couple of weeks."

"Am I?"

"Yes." Not planned, but it happened. "We're supposed to go shopping tomorrow and visit Portia on Sunday. I'd still like to do that together. What do you say?"

The pause seemed to last forever.

"Okay," Chantelle said finally.

Her answer wasn't a resounding yes, but he'd take it. This was his fault.

"Get some rest," he said. "I'll call in the morning before I go into the shop."

"Goodnight."

"Sweet dreams." Maybe she'd have a good one about him. He was going to need all the help he could get to make up for this.

He'd been an idiot for trying to keep his spending time with Chantelle a secret from his sisters. That wasn't fair to her. He was a grown man, one who could handle his mother.

He just needed to convince Chantelle to stay in Marietta for the remainder of the month. The question was…how?

Chapter Eleven

S TANDING OUTSIDE PORTIA'S hospital room on Sunday with York, Chantelle wondered why she'd agree to come today. Yes, she wanted to see Xavier, who'd been born late on Friday night, but shopping with York yesterday had been difficult. He'd said she was more than someone he was spending time with, but she didn't feel that way. If anything, she was more confused than ever.

She'd told Philippe she was leaving this week, but she wasn't sure when. She was on the wait list for a flight out of Bozeman on Tuesday, but could confirm a seat on Wednesday.

Should she or shouldn't she leave?

York kept trying to convince her to stay as long as he was in town.

Carrying a blue stuffed elephant that he'd claimed was a must buy when they went shopping, he looked way too adorable.

Chantelle adjusted the colorful tissue paper in the gift bag she held. Inside were footie pajamas, a set of burp cloths, and a board book.

"I'm going to knock," she said. "I don't want to intrude."

"Dakota said Portia wanted visitors. Since she decided not to give Xavier up for adoption, she wants to introduce her son to everyone."

"He looks like a cutie."

"Knock, so we can see him in person."

She did and was greeted by a "Come in."

York opened the door so she could walk in first. Portia lay in bed, holding a baby wrapped in a blanket against her chest.

"Happy Mother's Day!" Chantelle and York said at the same time.

"Hard to believe that's today." Portia grinned. "I thought I'd be celebrating as a mom-to-be this year, but this little guy decided he was tired of waiting another couple of weeks until his due date and wanted out. Meet Xavier. I call him Zavy."

"Cute name." Chantelle walked closer to the bed. "Original. Was Zavy named for someone in the family?"

Portia adjusted the baby's blue-and-pink-striped cap and then checked his swaddling blanket. "The name is an original, isn't it? He'll probably be the only Zavy in his class."

The baby was sleeping. Chantelle's chest tightened. "He's beautiful and so tiny."

"Congratulations," York said. "We have a couple of

things for Zavy."

"Thanks." Portia stared at her son with love. "He's being spoiled."

"As it should be." York placed the gifts on the wide window ledge next to two bouquets of flowers and other gift bags.

Portia looked at Chantelle. "Would you like to hold him?"

"Yes." The word flew from her mouth. "Let me wash my hands."

"Sage trains us well at the chocolate shop," York joked.

Portia laughed. "I miss that place."

York moved closer to the bed. "It'll be there when you're ready to come back. Until then, this little guy is going to take all your time."

"I'll be staying out at the Circle C Ranch for a while. Extra hands to help with a newborn."

Chantelle returned. "Good plan."

Portia handed her Zavy. Chantelle supported the newborn's head. She remembered that from a college friend who'd had a baby.

"He's so sweet." She couldn't believe how little he was. "And he's got that new baby smell."

"What smell?" York came toward her and sniffed. "Oh, that. Not bad."

Chantelle gave him a look. "It's delightful."

As she held Zavy, the longing for a family of her own

quadrupled. She'd thought about having kids someday, but she'd never felt that strong of a yearning for one of her own. Not until now.

"Can I have a turn?" York asked Portia after he'd washed his hands.

"Go ahead," she said.

Chantelle handed the baby to York. Some distance from the wee one would be good to keep her biological clock from going off even louder.

"Come here, little man." York said as he took the baby Chantelle offered. "Aren't you a handsome fellow? Bet you'll drive the girls crazy."

York gazed lovingly at Zavy.

Chantelle's stomach did one back spring after another. She had a feeling he would be the best uncle whenever his sisters had children, but she could picture him as a father also.

Her insides twisted and pulled as if someone were making taffy.

An image came into focus, one not so different from what was right in front of her. York holding his son...their son.

Oh, no.

No, no, no.

Her throat tightened.

She was falling for him.

They hadn't known each other that long, but it explained all her confusing feelings.

She was falling for York. She could picture their future together, one that could be amazing, but had no hope of happening because York wanted to travel, live out of a suitcase, and be free to do whatever.

A relationship was what she wanted, not him.

So where did that leave her? And them for as long as she was in town?

MONDAY, CHANTELLE WAS back at the shop. She hadn't said a word to York about her feelings for him because she was trying to figure out how she felt. It was hard. She wasn't sure if staying in Marietta to be with him for two more weeks was the right or the best decision for her.

All day, customers dropped off baby gifts for Zavy. Everyone wanted to see his pictures, and Sage, the proud great-aunt, was happy to oblige with a brag book she'd put together last night. Even though the shop closed in an hour, Sage was still there.

Spending so much time with the chocolatier was an enjoyable way for Chantelle to mark her last day helping at the shop. Dakota and Nevada had come by to have a hot chocolate this afternoon and sat at the far table.

Copper Mountain Chocolates was the place to be today.

The constant jingling of the bell continued.

"Welcome to Copper Mountain Chocolates," Chantelle

said.

A man in his early thirties walked in. His hair was light brown and curly. He carried a laptop bag on his shoulder. His suit and leather shoes looked expensive. She took a closer look. "Philippe?"

"Hello, cousin." Sometimes he spoke French to her, but not now.

She ran around the front of the counter and hugged him. "What are you doing here?"

"I was worried about you after our last phone call. I spoke with Father. He agrees it's time to bring you home."

Chantelle inhaled sharply. "To France? Really?"

"Yes, really." Philippe laughed. "How long until your shift ends?"

She glanced at the clock. "An hour."

"I've checked into the same hotel. We'll talk over dinner."

He looked around. That was when she noticed Dakota and Nevada staring from where they sat.

"A quaint shop," Philippe said. "Is York here?"

The two sisters exchanged a curious glance.

Chantelle shook her head. "He's off today."

Sage walked out from the back. "Sounds like a party in here."

"Sorry. My cousin just surprised me." Chantelle was still standing in front of the display case. "This is Philippe Delacroix. Philippe, this is Sage Carrigan O'Dell. She owns

Copper Mountain Chocolates. Dakota and Nevada Parker, York's sisters, are the ones at the table."

"The pleasure is mine, ladies." Philippe gave a slight bow. He might be a workaholic, but he had manners. "Chantelle has told me wonderful things about your shop and its delicious chocolates, Sage. I can't wait to try your single-origin bar."

Sage's smile spread. "Thank you. That's a customer favorite. Your cousin has been a tremendous help to us while another employee is on maternity leave."

"She has the chocolate touch," Philippe joked.

That earned him an elbow from Chantelle.

"Where are you from?" Sage asked.

Phillipe picked up a copper box of chocolates. "Bayonne, France."

"Delacroix." Sage's forehead creased. "Delacroix Chocolates?"

"My father is Laurent Delacroix," Philippe said without missing a beat.

"Chantelle is your cousin?" Sage asked.

Phillipe nodded. "Her mother, Marie, was my father's sister."

Sage looked at Chantelle. "You said the lavender-infused chocolate was your mother's recipe."

"Yes," Chantelle said. "I grew up making chocolates with her. She taught me everything I know."

"You might have picked up a few things at the chocolate

academy." Philippe's tone was lighthearted.

"Maybe a few." Chantelle smiled up at him.

"Why didn't you say anything about being a Delacroix?" Sage asked.

Chantelle shrugged. "I wanted to make a name for myself and earn respect on my own in the industry, not take advantage of my connection to Delacroix Chocolates. I've always gone by Cummings. That was my father's last name."

Sage's face paled. "Delacroix Chocolates has been buying recipes from independent chocolate producers."

"Yes," Philippe said. "But we won't tempt you with a purchase offer. I doubt we could afford your price."

"You couldn't, and the only way you'd know that is from your cousin." Sage pinned Chantelle with a glare. "You took this job to find out information on my shop."

Chantelle stiffened. "I helped out that first day because of Portia. You asked me to stay on."

Sage's lips narrowed. "Something I would have never done if I thought you'd be spying on my business."

"My cousin doesn't spy," Philippe countered. "She researches—"

"Semantics," Sage cut him off.

Chantelle didn't understand why Sage was so angry. "Normally, I visit a shop and do my research that way. But working here didn't give me any secret insider knowledge. I did have the opportunity to ask more questions, but I could have done that during a visit. You don't share your process or recipes with employees."

Sage's lips narrowed. "A good thing I don't or who knows what might have been passed on to Delacroix Chocolates."

Chantelle had to force air into her lungs. "I would never steal from you or anyone. Not ever."

"My cousin is not a thief. Delacroix Chocolates' recipes have been created in our laboratory or purchased legally for a more-than-fair price." Philippe's hand rested on Chantelle's shoulder. "My father and I were thrilled when Chantelle told us she'd be helping here. Not for your recipes, but because Copper Mountain Chocolate has a reputation for excellent customer service. All Delacroix factory employees are required to work in one of our retail stores to understand the importance of making a quality product. We felt her experience here would greatly benefit Chantelle."

"Please get Chantelle's things from her cubby," Sage said to Dakota, who made a beeline for the back. She returned with a purse and jacket.

Chantelle took the items and clutched them to her chest. "I wasn't trying to hurt you, Sage. I love working here. I didn't think my family mattered."

"It matters a lot." Sage took a deep breath. "You betrayed our trust and friendship by not telling us the truth about why you were here or who you really are.

Standing next to Sage, Dakota pursed her lips. "You should contact your attorney, Sage, and see what he thinks about this."

Chantelle's entire body tensed. "I don't understand."

Philippe put his arm around her. "Why would a lawyer get involved?"

Dakota stared down her nose at them. "Corporate, or perhaps this would be economic, espionage."

Chantelle's mouth gaped. She couldn't believe York's sister was saying this. About her.

"I didn't. I wouldn't." Chantelle dug her fingers into Philippe's arm.

Nevada walked over. "That's a serious charge, Dakota. Why don't we all take a step back for a minute?"

Chantelle found herself nodding.

"Espionage *is* a serious charge. As I said earlier, that is not how Delacroix Chocolates operates." The smile had vanished from Philippe's face. Hard lines now appeared. He stepped directly in front of Chantelle as if to shield her. "If anyone chooses to pursue this ridiculous claim, do know we are a billion-dollar multinational corporation with our own team of legal experts on staff. Making unfounded accusations against a well-respected company and an individual who is an industry expert will be costly."

Phillipe's sharp and precise tone made his threat clear: The Delacroix family had deep pockets. If anyone came after Chantelle or their company with an unfounded lawsuit, a countersuit would be filed. The legal fees would be astronomical.

"Please go," Sage said.

Chantelle glanced at Dakota, who glared at her, and then at Nevada, who offered a look of sympathy.

Philippe escorted Chantelle out of the shop. As the bell jingled, she felt a deep sense of loss. She'd thought of Copper Mountain Chocolates as a home away from home. And now...

Philippe kept his around her. "You're trembling."

"Sage and Dakota hate me."

"Emotions are running high. That's my fault. I should have waited until you were back at the hotel, but I wanted to see you."

"You're not the patient type."

"I should have been today. For your sake."

"Do you think Sage will listen to Dakota and call her lawyer?"

"No," he said without any hesitation. "I wasn't bluffing. We have the resources to drag out a lawsuit for years. Decades even. That was Dakota talking out of anger. She only works at the shop and was trying to present a united front with her boss. Don't worry. Sage is a smart business-woman. She won't be calling her lawyer. Even if she did, we have every report you've written. You may have had the opportunity to ask more questions at Copper Mountain Chocolates, but there is nothing confidential in what you provided us with."

"There isn't. I made sure of that."

"You still cannot return to the chocolate shop. No matter what reason you might have, it's not worth upsetting Sage and her staff. Do you understand?"

"I won't go back." Chantelle had no reason to return now. "I never meant to hurt anyone. I just wanted to do this on my own. Not rely on the Delacroix name."

"I know, and you did it on your own. Brilliantly. Father and everyone at Delacroix is proud of you and can't wait until you're in charge of the laboratory."

She froze. "What did you say?"

"Claude *finally* announced his retirement. It's what Father has been waiting for so he could bring you on without making a loyal employee, one who has been like a brother to him, feel pushed out. You seemed so eager to learn more and prove yourself, so Father let you. But there needs to be a transition period with you and Claude working together. That means we need to get you to Bayonne sooner rather than later."

"I-I don't know what to say."

"Not what you expected?"

"No, but thank you." Still, a weight pressed down on her shoulders.

"Thinking about York?"

She nodded. "I don't know what he's going to say given how Dakota feels. It's probably for the best. Uncle Laurent would never—"

"Father has no say in who you choose to date," Philippe

interrupted. "He just wants you to be happy. The same as I do."

"But my mother—"

"Our grandfather didn't forbid your mother from marrying your father. He only asked your mother that she and your father remain in Bayonne, but that wasn't acceptable to your father. He wanted to live in the United States."

Chantelle's mouth gaped. She closed it.

"You didn't know?" Philippe said.

Words wouldn't come. She shook her head.

"Your parents told the family to stay away from you, so we did. I'd never seen Father as happy as he was when you contacted him. He'd been trying to do what he could from afar."

Realization dawned. "The scholarship that came through at the last minute so I could finish college after my dad died."

Phillipe nodded. "Father has been planning for your return since then. It was all he could do to let you go back to America when you visited us. He missed his sister so much, but he wanted to make sure living in Bayonne and working at the chocolate factory were what you wanted. Of course, he also didn't want to hurt Claude, who stepped in after your mother left."

Chantelle's mind spun. "This is a dream come true. I wanted to prove myself and learn as much as I could."

"You have. In so many ways. I'm a bit jealous, to be honest, but I'll get over it."

"You'd better." A smile tugged at her lips. If only things could work out with York. Maybe they could. "I can't wait to put this behind me and move to Bayonne."

"There's no reason to wait."

"Weren't you going to try to be more patient?"

"Yes, but I can patiently arrange for movers to pack up your apartment while you finish up here. I'm assuming you need to speak with York."

"Yes, I do." Though she had no idea what she would say.

"I'll make some calls when we get back to the hotel."

She hugged him. "Thank you, Philippe."

"That's what family is for."

Yes, it is.

Chapter Twelve

Between Dakota and Nevada, York had an idea of what had happened at Copper Mountain Chocolates this afternoon. Dakota claimed Chantelle was a corporate spy who couldn't be trusted and wanted them to agree to never see her again. Nevada thought emotions were high and things would settle down with time and reflection.

York had no idea which sister was correct in her assessment or if both were wrong. Time to find out for himself.

At the Graff Hotel, he knocked on Chantelle's door.

She opened the door and motioned him into her room. "I'm so glad to see you."

"Is it true?" That sounded like the most logical question to start with.

"What?"

"That you're a Delacroix."

She took a breath. "My mother was a Delacroix, yes, and so am I."

Everyone knew Delacroix Chocolates. The blue-and-gold boxes were iconic. "Have you been spying for them?"

Hurt flashed in her eyes. "Is that what you think?"

"I have no idea, but Dakota is upset. Sage is, too. They feel betrayed. Lied to. And so do I." York shifted his weight between his feet. He was hoping she would cower a bit and beg his forgiveness for what she'd done. That didn't look likely. "You should have told me the truth about why you were in town."

As Chantelle stepped toward him, the quiver of her bottom lip told him she wasn't as strong as she appeared. "I came to Marietta to do a book signing and research Copper Mountain Chocolates for my uncle. This isn't the first time I've done that, but it's the first time I was asked to work at a shop. I only offered to help when Portia had to go to the hospital. Sage is the one who asked me to continue. I'm not a spy or a thief. Nothing in my report was confidential."

A part of him wanted to believe her the way Nevada did. His younger sister's logical mind had cut through the emotions and saw this as a failure to disclose information, not espionage. "You had the opportunity—"

"To what? Take pictures of the employees' binder? Because that's the only paperwork besides licenses and certificates in the shop."

"Did you copy the binder?"

Chantelle's mouth dropped open, and he regretted his question.

"Please tell me you're kidding," she said.

"I don't know how I feel. I thought I knew you, but then

I find out—"

"That I have family in France? I told you that. And that they were involved in chocolate. I only left off their name."

"That's the most important part," he said. "There's a fine line between research and spying when you're working for the competitor."

"Competitor?" She half-laughed. "I see you've taken Dakota's side on this. You do realize that Delacroix Chocolates is a multinational brand worth billions, don't you? Their competition isn't a small shop in a tourist town. They were only looking at buying recipes. Legally. And I don't work for them. Not yet anyway."

"But you will."

"Yes." Chantelle's gaze implored him. "I'm sorry you're upset. Sage and Dakota, too. That was never my intention. Everyone's acting like I put Sage's secret recipes on the internet. I didn't. Nor did I assume a fake identity or use a different name. I just didn't mention my family in France."

"That's enough."

"The only reason I stayed as long as I did was…"

"What?"

"You." Chantelle moistened her lips. "I liked helping out at the shop, but I wanted to spend more time with you."

A vice gripped his heart. "I want to believe you."

"Then believe me."

The muscles in York's shoulders knotted. The way her voice cracked on that last comment had him reaching out, but he drew back his arm. He couldn't be distracted.

York raised his chin. "I'm trying."

"Do you truly believe I'm capable of spying on Copper Mountain Chocolates?"

The question wasn't so easy to answer. He felt blindsided by what had happened and torn between Dakota and Chantelle. She'd been correct. He'd sided with his sister. Family first. What else could he do?

He took a breath and exhaled. The logical side of his brain seemed to be AWOL. "No. Yes. Maybe."

The anguish on her face hit him like a punch to his stomach.

Guilt tasted like dirt in his mouth.

Part of him felt as if he should have known what was going on, asked more questions, and kept those closest to him from feeling so betrayed. But he never could have imagined this scenario playing out.

Not with Chantelle.

The other part of him felt raw and achy because he had feelings for her. But what did that mean now? The connection between them was strong, but there was no commitment on either side. They hadn't known each other long, so what did she really owe him?

He brushed his hand through his hair. Trying to make logical sense out of this was impossible.

"I was hoping you wouldn't need proof, but here you go." Chantelle opened her laptop and pulled up a document.

"Note the date. I'd only worked at the shop for three days before I sent this to my uncle. You worked with me for two of those shifts. I was with Sage for the other."

He read the pages. Nothing was proprietary. No stolen recipes or product details. She hadn't included any photos. Her insights into the lack of a contingency plan should something happen to Sage were spot on, but far from secret. Everyone, including customers, knew Sage guarded her recipes and made all the products herself.

Chantelle crossed her arms over her chest. "Do you believe me now?"

"You didn't steal, but that doesn't make hiding your family connection right. You should have been honest."

"I'm sorry. I never meant to hurt anyone, especially you."

She moved closer and touched his face. Her hand felt so good on him. He wanted to lean in and forget everyone else.

"I...I care about you," she said with a voice full of emotion. "More than I thought possible, even though I know it's not what you want."

He cared about her, and she was right. He didn't want to feel that way about anyone. Not right now. "Dakota said you're moving to France."

A world away from him. A weight pressed on his chest. Breathing hurt. He'd known they'd be going their separate ways, but he hadn't wanted to think about it. Now, he didn't have a choice.

"Working there is a dream come true." Chantelle explained to him about her mother moving to America with her father and how Chantelle had reached out to the Delacroix family after her dad's death. "The extended Delacroix family lives around Bayonne where the corporate headquarters are located. I'll not only have a job, but a..."

"Family."

She nodded.

York knew that was important to her. "I get that part, but you didn't trust me with the truth. You told me pieces, but left off the most significant detail. You may not think you lied or did anything wrong, but everyone at the shop feels differently."

"Including you?"

He nodded. "I care about you, too."

There, he'd said it. So why didn't he feel better?

"If you care, then why did you need proof to believe I hadn't stolen information?"

A beat passed. And another.

He didn't—couldn't—answer because he hadn't wanted to believe her. "It doesn't matter. We were going to be saying goodbye soon enough anyway."

Her face fell. "There is a connection between us."

"One that has nowhere to go."

Her lip trembled again. "You said I wasn't someone you were just spending time with."

"I was wrong."

"Now who's being dishonest?" She blinked. Once, twice. "I see what you're doing."

"What?"

"You're using this as a reason to walk away."

"Yeah, right."

"Be honest." Her gaze didn't waver. "You admitted you care, but you have more feelings, too. Ones you don't want, so you're looking for a reason, an excuse to put an end to us, so you can be free to do whatever you want, whenever you want, with whomever you want."

She had lost it. He shook his head. *Big time.*

"You're reading way too much into a vacation romance," York said. "One that never had a chance of turning into something more. Did you really think we were going to end up together?"

She flinched as if he'd hit her. The raw hurt in her eyes made him wish he could take back his words, but it was too late.

Chantelle squared her shoulders and lifted her chin. "The romantic in me got carried away. I see that now. This was never going anywhere. It hardly had time to get started. I should have left Marietta as I planned and not stuck around."

His jaw twitched, his chest felt heavy, and his sinuses burned.

York looked for a sign she had doubts, regrets, anything, but that lower lip of hers no longer moved. She was steady and solid and no longer his.

He swallowed. "Then there's nothing left to say except goodbye."

With his heart pounding in his chest like a bass drum, he walked out of her room without looking back. The slam of the door punctuated the end of them.

The end.

York should be relieved it was over. Nothing would tie him down now. He would have the freedom he wanted.

Except…he hurt.

Not just his heart. All over. And badly.

But what else could he have said to her except goodbye?

As soon as the door closed, Chantelle leaned her back against the wall and slid to the floor in a heap.

His words swirled through her mind like a cyclone.

She hugged her knees, feeling as if her world had been turned upside down. Okay, not really. She'd only known York for a short time.

But she'd developed feelings for him.

Strong ones she'd never expected to feel. Different ones from what she'd ever felt before.

Love.

She was certain that was the only thing it could be.

She'd fallen in love with him.

It doesn't matter.

But it did to her.

He mattered.

Her eyes stung, but she blinked back the tears. Crying would only make her feel worse. She needed to get her things together so she could get out of Marietta. That would be her first step toward moving to France.

That was what she wanted.

France.

Her breath hitched.

Tears welled in her eyes.

Chantelle wanted York, too.

She looked up at the ceiling. That didn't stop her eyes from stinging. Blinking didn't stop the tears from falling.

She wiped her face.

Her fault.

She'd done this to herself. She hadn't believed she was doing anything wrong at the chocolate shop, but everyone else thought she had. Even though she'd known not to get involved romantically, she'd fallen in love with a man who wanted nothing to do with her.

Stupid.

That was what she'd been.

S-T-U-P-I-D.

Thank goodness she had her family. Chantelle was a Delacroix, and she'd finally found strength in that and in herself. She could get through anything, including a broken heart.

At least, she hoped so.

SITTING AT THE kitchen table, York rested his head on his hands. Sleep hadn't come last night. He was running on a mix of caffeine and sheer willpower.

No chocolate.

He wasn't sure he could eat another piece of the stuff. It reminded him too much of Chantelle.

Be honest. You admitted you care, but you have more feelings, too. Ones you don't want, so you're looking for a reason, an excuse to put an end to us, so you can be free to do whatever you want, whenever you want, with whomever you want.

Her words had been melded on his brain in a neverending audio loop he wanted to turn off, but couldn't. No matter how hard he tried.

"Hey." Dakota placed a plate of pancakes in front of him. "Eat something. Please."

"Thanks, but I'm not hungry."

She nudged the plate closer until he had to straighten. "Just a couple of bites. You didn't have dinner last night. I'm worried about you, and so is Nevada."

York took a bite but couldn't taste anything, not even the maple syrup. He might as well be eating paper. "Satisfied?"

"No." Concern clouded Dakota's eyes. She sat across from him. "I've never seen you like this."

He'd never felt this way before, not even when Jillian told him to keep his engagement ring. That she wouldn't leave her family in Texas and move to Maryland with him.

They'd dated for nearly a year. He'd known Chantelle for what? Almost two weeks?

But the length of time hadn't mattered. Like Adam in Fiji, York had fallen for Chantelle. That was the last thing he'd wanted to happen. He should be relieved it was over. Now he wouldn't have to figure out how to keep seeing her once they left Marietta.

Breaking up was a good thing.

Or should be.

Except a black hole resided where his heart should be.

Why?

Why couldn't he stop feeling this way?

That was something he couldn't reconcile.

"York."

The sound of Dakota's voice brought him back. "I'm fine."

She laughed. "Liar."

York ate another forkful of pancakes so he wouldn't have to talk. Chew. Swallow. Repeat. If he did that enough times, he'd finish everything on his plate.

His sister leaned over the table. "She lied to all of us. That hurts. I know you guys were friends."

She.

Chantelle.

Her name didn't bring a pang. He felt as if a drone had rammed into his chest and sent him plunging off a six-hundred-foot cliff. "She was way more than a friend."

"What?"

"We've been dating."

"How long?"

"Pretty much from the moment we met."

Dakota touched his arm. "Are you in love with her?"

His instinct was to say no. Except he couldn't.

"I…" York stared at what remained on his plate. "It doesn't matter."

She squeezed his forearm. "Of course it matters. Love trumps everything."

"Not family. Mine or hers."

Dakota dragged her teeth over her lower lip. "If you wanted to try—"

"You said I couldn't trust her." The words came out harsher than he'd intended.

Dakota's nose scrunched. "Maybe I shouldn't have said that. Yesterday was crazy. Emotions were out of control."

"They don't have to be today. Chantelle showed me the report she sent her uncle. She didn't steal anything from Sage. She would never do anything like that, but I didn't take her side in this. I didn't believe her. I needed proof."

"I had no idea you and Chantelle were that close."

Close as in spending time together. Holding hands. Kissing. That had been enough because there was more to come. Or so he'd thought.

"It doesn't matter," he repeated.

"You're miserable."

The word didn't begin to describe how he felt. "I'll get over it."

"Are you sure about that?" Dakota's worry was clear, but this time, he couldn't make his sister feel better.

Instead, York chose not to answer. He glanced at the clock on the microwave. "Thanks for breakfast. I have to get ready for work."

A day of pure torture to be surrounded by chocolate and not have Chantelle there.

"York."

"Not now." He stood and walked out of the kitchen.

Not ever.

⤚

IN HER HOTEL room, Chantelle packed her suitcase. The flights were still sold out, so her cousin had chartered a plane. That way, she could leave town today instead of tomorrow.

She folded her pink cardigan sweater. The last time she'd worn this was when they'd decided to be more than friends.

You're beautiful, smart, funny, and so many other things.

York's compliment had made her feel like the most special woman in the world. At least in his world. He'd been special to her, too, but now…

A lump burned in her throat. Her breath caught. Tears stung her eyes.

She blinked.

No more crying.

Chantelle clutched the sweater to her chest. Memories threatened to overwhelm her.

No.

Once she got back to her apartment, she could fall apart. Until then, she had to keep herself together. It would be a long day of traveling, and Philippe deserved a somewhat-sane travel companion. Being an emotional mess on the inside was one thing. Letting her cousin see that?

No way.

He'd seen enough last night.

She thought about tossing the sweater in the garbage can, but shoved it and a pair of jeans in her suitcase instead.

A knock sounded on her door.

Chantelle hadn't called for a bellhop, and Philippe said he'd text before he came over.

She checked the peephole, but only saw a woman with brown hair. Must be housekeeping. Though she thought she'd put the *Do Not Disturb* sign out. She opened the door.

Dakota and Nevada Parker stood there.

Chantelle gripped the door handle. Her throat tightened.

The two women weren't smiling. If anything, they looked tense. Exactly how she felt right now.

She opened her mouth to speak, but no words came.

"Do you have a minute?" Dakota asked.

Talking was the last thing Chantelle wanted to do, but a part of her was curious about why the two were here. She couldn't imagine York sent them.

Chantelle took a breath and then another. "I have a minute."

Nevada looked to her left and right. "Can we come in?"

Chantelle opened the door wider in a silent invitation.

The two sisters walked in.

The room was a disaster area. Two pillows were on the floor. Her suitcase lay open on top of the tangled sheets on the bed. Clothes were piled next to it.

To be honest, Chantelle didn't care. She had a feeling the room looked better than she did.

She stood by the dresser and crossed her arms over her chest.

Nevada looked at Dakota, who took a deep breath.

Tension filled the room.

Chantelle's patience disappeared. "If you have something to say, please say it. I need to finish packing."

"York is miserable," Dakota said.

"You don't look too great yourself," Nevada added.

Chantelle shrugged. At least she wasn't the only one suffering, but that feeling was short-lived. She didn't want York to be miserable and feel the way she did. Chantelle wouldn't wish that on her worst enemy. She wanted him to be happy and have a giant, heart-melting smile on his face.

Because of her.

Not. Going. To. Happen.

She raised her chin. "There's nothing I can do about that."

"That's why we're here." Regret filled Dakota's words. "To see if we can help."

"I think you've done enough." Chantelle tried to keep any bitterness she might feel out of her voice. She wasn't sure she succeeded.

"I needed to support Sage. Help her. I was hurt. Angry. But now I...we...have to try," Dakota said. "I've never seen York like this. He's not eating."

Nevada nodded. "Or sleeping. He won't talk to us about it."

The words "not my problem" were on the tip of Chantelle's tongue, but she couldn't say them. "Once he starts his new job, he'll be so busy he won't have time to think about anything. He'll be back to his old self before you know it."

Dakota shook her head. "I don't think so. This is different. He's never not talked to us about stuff. I think—"

"We think York is in love with you," Nevada blurted.

Dakota glared at her sister.

"What?" Nevada shrugged. "It needed to be said."

No, it didn't.

Chantelle could barely breathe. She forced air into her lungs. "I know you care about your brother, but York is not in love with me."

If he was, he would have trusted her without needing proof. He would have never walked away from her the way he did.

"He's a great guy, but whatever was between us is over. And that's for the best." Somehow, she managed to keep her tone steady. "My cousin and I are flying to Boston today. We'll pack up my things there, and then go on to France to be with my family."

She stumbled on the last word because York felt like family. "I need to finish packing."

"Talk to him, please," Dakota urged. "Even if it's just to say goodbye again."

Chantelle was tempted, except it might make her heart hurt more. "We've said our goodbyes."

"Doing this might give you and him better closure," Nevada said.

"And if it doesn't?" Chantelle asked.

Dakota opened her mouth.

"You can relocate to France and not have to wonder 'what if,'" Nevada said before her sister could answer.

Nevada was smart, and what she said made sense, but Chantelle wasn't ready to say yes. "I need to finish packing. I'll see if I have time when I'm done."

That was as much as she was willing to commit.

Was seeing York again going to make a difference? What if his sisters were wrong? What if he didn't want to see her? But what if he did?

"Is he at your house?" she asked Dakota.

"He's working at the chocolate shop this morning."

Chantelle's heart fell. "I'm sorry, but I can't go back there. I promised Philippe I wouldn't because it would only upset Sage."

Chapter Thirteen

A LITTLE BEFORE ten o'clock, York arrived at the chocolate shop. This was normally Dakota's day to work, but she would be coming in later. A pot of hot chocolate simmered on the burner behind the counter and filled the store with the most amazing aroma, as usual.

Everything was the same as it had been except for one thing. The place seemed different without Chantelle's smiling face next to him.

He went into the kitchen area to grab an apron. "Good morning."

Sage stood at a table pouring chocolate into flower-shaped molds. Those had been big sellers for Mother's Day, but continued to be popular for gifts and wedding favors. The fact he knew that told him how far he'd come since his first day at the shop with Chantelle.

"You look tired. Get any sleep last night?" Sage asked.

No, but he wasn't about to tell his boss that. "A little."

Maybe an hour or so. He'd spent most of the night tossing and turning. The hurt on Chantelle's face was etched on his brain. Nothing would take it away.

He put on an apron. "I'll get everything ready out front."

"York," Sage called.

He turned.

"You and Chantelle seemed close," Sage said. "That doesn't just go away after you say goodbye."

He nodded. The problem was no one knew how close he and Chantelle had gotten. And he'd liked it that way. No pressure from his mom or questions from his sisters or gossip from any of the nosy folks around town.

Though she'd told her family about him. That had surprised York, but he had no doubt her feelings for him had been real.

He also knew she hadn't been spying. Yes, he'd seen the proof, but he should have known better than to ask. That wasn't the kind of person Chantelle Cummings was. Even though she'd done everything she could to help them, everyone she'd met here believed the worst of her.

Including him.

York was used to things going from one step to the next. If something didn't work, he debugged the line of code and moved on. It was a plan that made logical sense.

Nothing about Chantelle made sense.

She was impossible to figure out.

The bell on the door jingled.

He smiled. "Welcome to Copper Mountain Chocolates."

A young couple ordered two hot chocolates to go. As he

prepared the drinks, York hoped this would be a busy day so the time would go faster.

He'd only been here a few minutes, but he wanted his shift to be over. This would be his last day now that Rosie was back in town. The end couldn't come soon enough.

As he stirred the pot of hot chocolate on the burner, the bell on the door jingled.

He forced a smile. "Welcome to Copper Mountain Chocolates."

The greeting was automatic, and he hoped he sounded friendly. He'd given up all hopes of being cheery.

His sisters entered the shop.

"Hey," Nevada said.

Dakota remained silent.

"What are you doing here?" he asked.

Neither said anything.

Uh-oh. His sisters were never silent unless…

"What did you do?" he tried again.

Dakota blew out a breath. "We went to see Chantelle."

What? He clutched the edge of the counter. "Why?"

"To see if she'd come to the shop and talk to you before she left Marietta," Dakota said.

His breath caught, and his heart stilled. He didn't want his sisters involved in this, but he had to know. Ask. "What did she say?"

"Her cousin told her she can't come back to the shop," Nevada answered.

Dakota rubbed the back of her neck. "I got the feeling she wouldn't have come even if she could."

Nevada nodded. "Me, too. But she looks as bad as you do."

His chest felt as if it might burst. "Thanks for trying. It's over."

Nevada took a step forward. "But—"

"No buts." He hadn't thought his heart could hurt any more, but it did. "Let this drop. Don't mention *her* again. Go. I need to work."

"No." Dakota's forceful tone shocked him. "You're the one who needs to go—to the Graff to see Chantelle before she's gone. She and her cousin are flying to Boston today. They'll pack up her apartment and move her to France."

"That's what she wants."

"She wants you," Nevada countered.

He shook his head.

"Trust me, I've been there," Nevada said.

Dakota nodded. "Me, too."

"No. I won't go over there." York didn't know if it was his pride or stubbornness or a combination of the two that wouldn't let him consider it. "Why should I be the one to give in and go to her when she doesn't want to come to me?"

"Because when you love someone, you either both win or you both lose if you fight," Nevada said in a tone that made her sound older and wiser than both he and Dakota. "It's not giving in when you're in this together."

Dakota pointed to their not-so-baby sister. "What she said."

Nevada continued. "If you hadn't called me on Valentine's Day, I'm not sure I would have left Dakota's house. Who knows what would have happened with Dustin if I hadn't? He had this whole grand gesture planned, but he didn't know if I would show up to see it. I'm so thankful I did, because I don't want to consider us not being together."

The emotion in his sister's voice tugged at his heart. He remembered that phone call. Dakota had let him know just how terrible things were, so he'd hung up from her call and phoned Nevada right away.

"Things would have worked out. You love Dustin." He looked at Dakota. "And you're in love with Bryce."

"I know that now, but I wasn't sure of anything back then. The situation seemed so hopeless," Dakota admitted. "I was confused and a complete wreck. If Bryce hadn't made the effort, we wouldn't be together today."

York let the words sink in. "You think I need to make the effort."

"If you love her," Dakota said.

He took a breath and thought for a moment. "I don't know how I feel."

"Are you sure about that?" Nevada stared up at him. "Because Chantelle is only a couple of blocks away. That's a little closer than having a freaking ocean between you."

He hesitated. "I don't know what I'd say."

"Just say your sisters made you do it," Nevada said in a strong, but matter-of-fact tone. A voice she likely used with her freshman students to make them do what she wanted.

That wasn't going to work on him. "I can't say that, but maybe..."

"Maybe?" Dakota asked.

"Maybe." That was as much as he had, but an idea popped into his head.

He grabbed a flower-shaped chocolate lollipop. If he couldn't think of anything to say, he could hand her the flower and say it was for her flight. Stupid, but better than standing there like a silent fool. Which was a distinct possibility.

As was having her slam the door in his face.

But that was a chance he had to take. "Could one of you cover the cost of this?"

Nevada reached into her purse. "I will."

Dakota darted into the back. Thirty seconds later, she came out putting on an apron. "I'll cover here."

Was he really going to do this? All the reasons he shouldn't filled his brain. "I—"

She walked around the counter and gave him a shove. "Go. Now."

Nevada held the door open. "Hurry. It didn't look like Chantelle had much left to pack."

York didn't know why this mattered so much to his sisters. "This is going to explode in my face."

"Maybe," Dakota said. "But maybe it won't, and at least you'll know."

"Know what?" he asked.

"That going over there was the right choice," Nevada said.

He walked out the door with a mix of apprehension and futility. Chantelle wanted to be in France with her family. That was the only thing that mattered to her now. He'd blown his chance.

Turn around.

York ignored the voice and kept walking. Yes, she wanted to move to France, but he'd never given her another option. Something was driving him toward Front Avenue.

Be honest. You admitted you care, but you have more feelings, too. Ones you don't want, so you're looking for a reason, an excuse to put an end to us, so you can be free to do whatever you want, whenever you want, with whomever you want.

Dakota and Nevada were correct. He needed to talk to Chantelle again.

He picked up his pace.

Thoughts bounced around as if his head were a pinball machine. Random images, feelings, and memories. Words formed, jumbled and confused.

Maybe he could tell Chantelle that spending the past couple of weeks with her had been wonderful. He'd spent many of the days working at the shop, but his time with her had been the best. He had no regrets except he wished things had turned out differently between them.

Maybe saying those words would give them better closure to begin the next part of their lives.

Without each other.

His heart seized.

No.

He didn't want to be without her.

He...

An image of her formed. One of her the first time he'd seen her at the bookstore. The pretty blonde in the fancy blue suit who was nervous but didn't want anyone to know. Another image appeared. Of her making a bouquet of chocolate flowers for a husband to give his wife. The look of awe on her face when she held Portia's baby. The way Chantelle looked at him with a smile on her face and affection in her eyes. That look made him feel like he could do anything. With her next to him, he was invincible.

I...

I love her.

Everything they'd gone through, all the feelings and things he couldn't quite understand, seemed to suddenly make sense.

York broke into a run.

He had no idea how Chantelle felt, but that didn't matter. He needed to tell her what she meant to him. It might not change anything...or it could change everything.

Please don't let me be too late.

WHERE WAS THE bellhop?

Pacing in front of the window, Chantelle glanced at the digital clock on the nightstand. She and Philippe would have plenty of time to make the drive to the airport, but for her peace of mind, she wanted to get out of Marietta.

The more she thought about it, the more she realized Dakota and Nevada were wrong about their brother's feelings. York had walked away. He was the one who didn't want a relationship with Chantelle, and not because she'd spied or lied or whatever everyone at the chocolate shop had decided she'd done.

Okay, she'd called him out. She'd said harsh words after being hurt. Chantelle hated that she'd done that, but self-preservation had kicked in. She couldn't stop herself.

It was good she couldn't go to the chocolate shop.

Her heart couldn't take more rejection or sadness. And that was all she would find at Copper Mountain Chocolates. She needed to get far, far away from Marietta, Montana and never come back.

A knock sounded on the door.

Thank goodness. The bellhop was finally here.

She hurried to the door and opened it.

Not the bellhop.

Her mouth gaped. She closed it. "York..."

He stood in the doorway with an anxious expression on his face. Stubble covered his cheeks. His eyes were red. His lids were heavy.

"You're still here." The relief in his voice was palpable. The corners of his mouth turned upward.

What was going on? She wanted to ask, but she pressed her lips together instead. No way did she trust her voice. Or herself.

The door handle dug into her palm.

"May I come in?" he asked.

Chantelle hated how bad he looked because she could be staring in a mirror. She cleared her dry throat. "I'm waiting for the bellhop to get my luggage. Philippe and I are leaving."

"What I have to say won't take long."

A part of her was happy to see York. She didn't like that part. Worse, she fought the urge to reach out and touch him. To feel his skin, his warmth, so she could know she wasn't daydreaming. Instead, she motioned him inside.

He walked to the center of the room.

She stayed by the door. Silly, yes, but self-preservation wouldn't let her move closer to him. She wasn't looking forward to another goodbye. Nervously, she rubbed her damp palms against her jeans.

York took a breath and pulled something from the front pocket of his apron. He handed her a flower-shaped dark chocolate treat tied with a pink ribbon. "For you."

"This isn't necessary."

Shrugging, he shoved his hands in his jean pockets. "Eat it on the flight."

"The flight," she repeated. "Thanks for the chocolate. I need you to leave."

"I need you to stay."

Feeling off-balance, she leaned against the wall to steady herself and narrowed her gaze. "What? Why?"

"I love you."

No way did he just say that. Chantelle squinted as if her eyes could help her hear better. "What?"

He hesitated. "I…I love you."

Her insides trembled. She'd longed for someone to say those three words to her—she'd hoped it would be him—but she was afraid to believe him. It was too hard after everything that had happened.

She raised her chin. "That's not what you said before."

"I'm sorry. I didn't realize it before. It wasn't until today on my way over here. I'm much better at debugging code than figuring out my own feelings. You were correct. I was looking for an excuse to call things off." He brushed his hand through his hair. "Forgive me."

"I want to, but—"

"I get it." His eyes brimmed with understanding and affection. "I was an idiot. I can't take back what happened. I wish I could, but that doesn't change the fact that I love you."

Her resolve was melting like a chocolate bar on a sunny day.

"I know you want to be part of a family." He squeezed

her hand. "Let's be a family."

The air whooshed from her lungs. She tried to speak, but she couldn't.

"I hurt you, but I'll do what I can to make it up to you. You and your happiness are the most important things right now. I just couldn't see it, but I promise not to be such an idiot in the future. If you'll let me."

Each word was breaking through her walls like a missile making a direct hit on its target. She couldn't take much more.

"York, please." The words were painful to say. "I wish things were different. I really do, but my family—"

"I can't give you blood relatives or a job at a fancy chocolate factory, but I will gladly give you my heart. And Parker might not sound as fancy as Delacroix, but it's a good solid name."

"Wait...what?" She tilted her head. "Parker?"

"I'm rushing, but I can't lose you. Last night and this morning have been the worst ever. But it took thinking I might not see you again to make me hope for a different ending. A happy one."

"And you just figured this all out?"

He nodded. "Amazing what sheer panic and a walk can do to clear a guy's mind."

She wasn't sure what to think. He was saying the right words and staring at her with love in his gaze, but something held her back. "You want to travel, see the country, be free—"

"That was before. Now I want the woman with the chocolate touch. I want you, Chantelle. I wanted you the moment you crashed into me, but I didn't know how much I needed you until today." He laced his fingers with hers. "I don't care where we end up—France is fine—as long as we're together. The next six months will be difficult, since I'm locked into a contract, but after that, I want us to be together."

Chantelle was scared, but she knew what her heart— what *she*—wanted. Finally, she realized why her mother had made the choice she had and understood it in a way she couldn't before. Chantelle's situation wasn't the same. She had her uncle and cousin's love and support. They wanted her in Bayonne, and that was where she wanted to be.

But without York with her, it wouldn't feel right.

Philippe said Uncle Laurent would support whatever she wanted. She hoped so.

There was only one decision, one choice, she could make.

York.

Her heart thumping like mad, she stared up at him. "I love you, too."

Relief crossed his face…followed by a satisfied smile that reached the corners of his eyes. He pulled her into his arms and kissed her hard on the lips.

A possessive kiss.

One that staked his claim.

She didn't mind because the way she kissed him back said one thing—*mine*.

My love.

My family.

She did have the chocolate touch. Chocolate had brought her everything she'd dreamed about and a little extra, too—York.

Chocolate with Chantelle

*T*HIS IS IT!

For several years, I've explored the world of chocolate. I've enjoyed sharing my discoveries with reviews and articles, so it's a bittersweet moment as I write my final blog post.

My late mother, Marie Delacroix Cummings, taught me everything she knew about chocolate in a small kitchen near Boston. She knew a lot because she was a chocolatier for Delacroix Chocolates, her family's company. She gave up that job and left France to move to the United States to be with my father, but that didn't stop her from passing on her passion for chocolate to me.

I'm delighted to announce that I've accepted a position with Delacroix Chocolates in Bayonne, France. This is not only an opportunity of a lifetime from a career standpoint, but more importantly, the move will also allow me to live closer to my family. That's something I've missed since the death of my father.

I kept the fact I was a part of the Delacroix family a secret because I didn't want to use their connections and reputation to further my career in the industry. I also made a conscious decision to not review any Delacroix product or store. Some may feel misled or betrayed in some way. I'm sorry if you are one of the people who do. Perhaps I was naïve to think being a Delacroix didn't matter, but it has never been my intention to hurt anybody, and I apologize if I did.

Before I sign off, I have one last recommendation for all the chocolate lovers to check out. There's a fabulous small-batch producer called Copper Mountain Chocolates located in Marietta, Montana on Main Street.

If you get the chance to visit, do. The owner, Sage Carrigan O'Dell, has created delicious, handcrafted chocolates. The shop's welcoming atmosphere will make you feel like a regular even if it's your first visit.

The seventy-two-percent Criollo bar is to die for and my favorite product of theirs. The tasting I attended left me wanting more. My mouth was a buffet of flavors, including a surprising caramel and banana, that you won't want to miss. The selection of truffles will satisfy any chocoholic, but if you're only going to order one, I recommend the champagne. You won't be disappointed. The hot chocolate—Sage's secret recipe—is a creamy mixture topped with whipped cream and shaved chocolate. After one mug, you'll find yourself wanting another. One of the retail staff calls it a chocolate lover's ambrosia. I agree!

I had the pleasure of working behind the counter at Copper Mountain Chocolates for a brief time. Writing about chocolate and selling it are two different things. The staff at the shop taught me so much about customer service...and life. The experience has changed me. For the better, I hope!

I learned family isn't always related by blood. Often, people can be related by a shared interest. In the case of the shop, it was chocolate. The customers' enthusiasm for Sage's masterpieces was contagious, as was the staff's. I was fortunate to work with another newbie at the shop, as well. Between working together and exploring the town of Marietta, I fell hard for him. The last thing I expected to find was love at the chocolate shop, but I'm so grateful I did.

As for the ending to my story, let's hope for happily ever after.

Chantelle

Epilogue

November

CHANTELLE COULDN'T BELIEVE Bryce and Dakota's wedding reception was over. Time had flown by with dancing, eating, and drinking. Such fun. The happy newly-weds had left a half hour ago to a secret honeymoon destination—one that not even Walt Grayson knew about.

York wrapped his arms around Chantelle. He looked so handsome in his tuxedo, and she couldn't help but imagine him as a groom someday in the future. They were taking things slow right now.

Although maybe that would happen sooner than she thought. She *had* caught the bridal bouquet.

"Great wedding," he said.

"Perfect." Just like this time together with him.

They'd promised the bride and groom to stay until everyone was gone. The other guests had left. That included Nevada, Dustin, and York's parents, who were not only nice, but also treated Chantelle like one of the family.

"Your parents looked so proud and happy today."

"Not just because of Dakota and Bryce's wedding." York gave her a squeeze. "The colonel thinks you're the bee's knees."

"Yeah, right."

"I'm not kidding. He likes you so much he didn't mention me leaving the air force once."

"That has nothing to do with me. You're killing it as a consultant."

"How would you know that?" York asked.

She kissed his cheek. "Because I know you."

"You're biased."

"Maybe a little."

He laughed. "My mom likes you, too."

"She's great." Mrs. Parker had peppered Chantelle with questions. Meddlesome, eh…maybe a little. But she didn't mind. The woman was only doing it because she wanted her three children to be happy. York, Dakota, and Nevada were lucky to have a mom who cared so much. "Your parents are nice. I enjoyed meeting them."

"We both like each other's family. That's a good sign."

She hoped so.

The DJ packed up his equipment. Servers cleared the remaining glasses and cake plates from tables. The wedding coordinator made a sweep to see if any items had been left.

York ran a hand through Chantelle's hair. "I'm glad it's just you and me right now. I enjoyed today, but I'm tired of making small talk."

"Me, too."

She leaned against him. Her sense of belonging and love had only intensified over the past six months. The distance between them hadn't been easy, but his frequent-flier mileage was adding up. They'd managed a few visits, including one courtesy of her uncle for a birthday surprise.

The time apart hadn't been all bad. She'd gotten to know her family and felt as if she'd truly come home. She and York had gotten to know each other better via online chats and phone calls. The months away from him had given her a clearer appreciation and understanding of what they had and how good that could be when they were together again.

York nuzzled against her neck. His kisses were lethal, but in an enjoyable way.

She tipped her head back to give him better access. "Ohh."

"You like that?" He nibbled on her earlobe. "How about this?"

"Mmm-hmm."

"There will be more of that later."

"Tease."

Laughing, he let go of her and picked up the bouquet sitting on the table next to them. A long ribbon hung from the flowers' handle, so he tied it into a neat bow. "Nice catch."

"After Nevada and Dustin eloped to Niagara Falls, I

think Dakota was aiming for me or her bridesmaid Kelly, who was standing next to me."

"I'd put money on you."

Chantelle sniffed the sweet roses. She'd been thrilled when the bouquet landed unexpectedly in her hands, even though she hadn't been trying like some of the others. Still, she didn't want York to feel any pressure. They hadn't been together long, and most of that time had been apart.

"It's a fun tradition," she said. "But a little silly."

He stiffened. "Does that mean you don't want to get married next?"

"I…" Her pulse felt as if afterburners had been turned on. Chantelle looked up at him. She didn't see his lopsided smile or the glint in his eyes he usually had when he was teasing. "Are you asking?"

"Maybe."

"Yeah, right." She laughed it off because he had to be joking. She wanted that eventually, but no need to rush things. "Like either of us wants a long-distance marriage."

As he ran the edge of his fingertip along her jawline, sparks of pleasure shot through her. "I'm tired of being apart."

She wanted York in her life. If long distance was the only way, so be it. "It's better than nothing."

"True, but I'm almost through my six-month probation period. That means I can transfer. There's an opening in our Europe operations. I'm going to apply. And if I don't get it,

I'll keep trying."

Her lips parted. "We'd be on the same continent."

"Better than that."

She was afraid to hope. "Same country?"

He nodded. "I'd still be traveling, but I could make Bayonne my home base."

She shimmied with excitement. "Yes!"

York laughed, a sound that wrapped around her heart and squeezed tight. "To my applying for a transfer?"

"Yes to that and everything else that might come with your transfer." She lost herself in his gaze. "I love you."

"More than chocolate?"

Chantelle tilted her chin as if she had to ponder the question.

He brushed his lips over her hair. "Don't make me suffer."

"Way more than chocolate."

His gaze darkened. "You're in charge of Delacroix's chocolate laboratory. You sure about that?"

"Positive." She traced the outline of his lips with her finger. The man was gorgeous, but he was so much more than a pretty face. He was a good, kind-hearted, loving man. She kissed him hard on the mouth. "Satisfied now?"

"For now, but I'll want you to show me how much more later."

She grinned. "That can be arranged."

"How about showing me every day after that?"

Chantelle stared up into hazel eyes she knew better than her own. In them, she saw her future. Her family. Her happily ever after. Together with his.

"Every single day," she said. "No matter what."

She kissed him again. A kiss that spoke of her promise to do that. That hinted at the life they would share together. A kiss that was…better than chocolate?

Oh, yeah.

The End

You'll love the next book in…

The Love at the Chocolate Shop series

Love blooms in and around the Copper Mountain Chocolate shop of Marietta, Montana in a twelve book series featuring authors C.J. Carmichael, Melissa McClone, Debra Salonen, Roxanne Snopek, Marin Thomas and Steena Holmes.

Book 1: *Melt My Heart, Cowboy* by C.J. Carmichael

Book 2: *A Thankful Heart* by Melissa McClone

Book 3: *Montana Secret Santa* by Debra Salonen

Book 4: *The Chocolate Cure* by Roxanne Snopek

Book 5: *The Valentine Quest* by Melissa McClone

Book 6: *Charmed by Chocolate* by Steena Holmes

Book 7: *The Chocolate Comeback* by Roxanne Snopek

Book 8: *The Chocolate Touch* by Melissa McClone

Book 9: *Sweet Home Cowboy* by Marin Thomas

Book 10: Coming soon by Debra Salonen

About the Author

USA Today Bestselling author **Melissa McClone** has published over twenty-five novels with Harlequin and been nominated for Romance Writers of America's RITA award. She lives in the Pacific Northwest with her husband, three school-aged children, two spoiled Norwegian Elkhounds and cats who think they rule the house. For more on Melissa's books, visit her website: www.melissamcclone.com.

Thank you for reading

The Chocolate Touch

If you enjoyed this book, you can find more from all our great authors at TulePublishing.com, or from your favorite online retailer.

TULE
PUBLISHING

Made in the USA
Columbia, SC
16 October 2021